KT-461-782

City and Islington Sixth Form College
283-309 Goswell Road
London
EC1
020 7520 0601 0052

CITY AND ISLINGTON
COLLEGE

This book is due for return on or before the date last stamped below.
You may renew by telephone. Please quote the Barcode No.
May not be renewed if required by another reader.

Fine: 5p per day

7 DAY
BOOK

LONGMAN
YORK PRESS

YORK PRESS
Immeuble Esseily, Place Riad Solh, Beirut.

ADDISON WESLEY LONGMAN LIMITED
Edinburgh Gate, Harlow,
Essex CM20 2JE, England
Associated companies, branches and representatives
throughout the world

First published 1980
Eleventh impression 1998

ISBN 0-582-78107-8

Produced by Addison Wesley Longman Singapore Pte Ltd
Printed in Singapore

Contents

Part 1

Introduction

Jane Austen's life and times

The author of *Sense and Sensibility* was born in 1775 in Steventon, a village in southern England. The younger daughter (and youngest child) of a country clergyman, she had six brothers, one of whom was adopted by a wealthy kinsman and succeeded in time to his family name of Knight and also to his house and property named Godmersham, in Kent. Two of the Austen boys, Frank and Charles, rose to become Admirals in the Navy. Another, Henry, became a clergyman. Jane Austen's elder sister, Cassandra, remained (like Jane) unmarried and outlived her. Although many events of importance occurred during her lifetime (including the American and French Revolutions, the Reign of Terror in France during which the husband of one of her cousins was executed, the meteoric rise to power of Napoleon Bonaparte, and the naval battles of Lord Horatio Nelson), her novels do not draw their materials from any of these sources. Although English literature itself was in these years undergoing a period of transition from the eighteenth-century values and techniques of Pope and Dr Johnson to new, 'romantic' ideas and methods popularised by Sir Walter Scott, William Wordsworth and Lord Byron, Jane Austen lived her life outside the English literary world and is not known to have ever met a fellow author. Until she was twenty-five years old she lived in her father's rectory. In 1800 the family moved to Bath and, on the death of the Reverend George Austen in 1806, to Southampton. In 1809 Mrs Austen and her two daughters settled at Chawton Cottage, a small house on Edward Knight's Hampshire property, and here Jane Austen lived until within a few weeks of her death in 1817. Here too all her completed novels were put by her into their final form and prepared for publication.

With her brothers and their families, and with her sister Cassandra, Jane Austen enjoyed a close, affectionate relationship and maintained an intimate correspondence. She distributed the greater part of her life between Hampshire and visits to Bath, Kent and London. Her family was her first and most appreciative audience, and the reading public she envisaged for *Sense and Sensibility* was clearly very like her parents and her brothers and sisters in its tastes: cultured, lively, humorous, and scornful of false pomp and pretentiousness. She began to write as a young child, scribbling playlets and little satirical stories and sketches for the amusement of her family. The Austens enjoyed theatricals and in these family diversions she probably first exercised the skill she displays in handling dramatic dialogue (see the conversation between John and Fanny Dashwood in Volume I, Chapter 2, and Mrs Jennings's breathless account of happenings at the Dashwoods' house in Volume III, Chapter 1) and the taste for ambiguous comedy of situation that directs the presentation of events in Volume III, Chapters 3 and 4. The ridiculous and unnatural elements in contemporary literature amused the Austens and tempted Jane Austen in the direction of satire: a 'History of England' she wrote at the age of sixteen satirically imitates the style and content of contemporary history books, and readers of *Sense and Sensibility* can easily trace a resemblance between the romantic absorption in each other that makes Marianne and Willoughby 'most exceedingly laughed at' (Volume I, Chapter 11) and two characters in a sketch written in 1790 titled 'Love and Freindship' who took 'due care to inform the surrounding Families, that as their Happiness centred wholly in themselves, they wished for no other society'.

Except for a brief period during which Cassandra and Jane Austen were sent to a boarding school in Reading, their education was conducted at home under their father's supervision. He gave tuition to a few selected pupils every year, and encouraged his own daughters to read widely. Jane Austen's reading for pleasure included the works of Shakespeare, Pope, Dr Johnson, Goldsmith, Cowper and Crabbe. She knew the poetry of Scott and Byron, and read with admiration the novels of Fanny Burney, Maria Edgeworth, Henry Fielding and Samuel Richardson. The sentimental fiction of Henry Mackenzie and Charlotte Smith, and the 'Gothic' terror-novels of Horace Walpole and Anne Radcliffe were also very well known to her, as may be judged from her satire of sentimentality and sensationalism in both *Sense and Sensibility* and *Northanger Abbey*. Like most girls of their station in life, she and Cassandra learned French and Italian, and were taught to sing, play musical instruments, sew and embroider (a patchwork quilt completed by the two girls, which must have involved many hours of labour and much patience, may be seen among other 'relics' of Jane Austen's life preserved at Chawton Cottage to this day). She was very fond of dancing, enjoyed making and wearing pretty clothes in her youth, and when her family's income decreased after her father's death practised the domestic skills that make a little money go a long way. Jane Austen described herself once in a letter as 'the most unlearned and uninformed female who ever dared to be an authoress', but like others among her ironic statements we need not take this too seriously.

Jane Austen's social circle was restricted to members of her own rank, the 'genteel' upper middle class. As a girl she attended balls and monthly assemblies, and was taken visiting, to tea-parties, card-parties, musical evenings, dinner-parties and theatricals. Her authorship was kept, by her own wish, a family secret. Chawton society was very limited, as her letters make clear, and Jane Austen probably did not wish to be singled out and even, perhaps, avoided by her neighbours as being dangerously 'satirical' (Lady Middleton's objection to Elinor and Marianne Dashwood's visiting her). Her circumstances as a writer are described in her nephew's *Memoir*: sharing a bedroom with her sister, and living in a cottage (we might compare it to Barton Cottage in *Sense and Sensibility*):

> She had no separate study to retire to; and most of the work must have been done in the general sitting-room, subject to all kinds of casual interruptions. She was careful that her occupation should not be suspected by servants, or visitors, or any person beyond her own family party. She wrote upon small sheets of paper which could easily be put away, or covered with a piece of blotting-paper. There was, between the front door and the offices, a swing-door which creaked when it was opened; but she objected to having this little inconvenience remedied, because it gave her notice when anyone was coming.

Jane Austen's relationship with her sister Cassandra is very likely to have influenced her presentation of Elinor and Marianne, and indeed of the many pairs of similarly contrasted heroines that appear in novel after novel. On her death, Cassandra wrote: 'I *have* lost a treasure, such a Sister, such a friend as never can have been surpassed—she was the sun of my life, the gilder of every pleasure, the soother of every sorrow.' The loving concern with which Elinor watches over her wayward sister, her capacity to feel for her in her troubles and forget her own sorrows in Marianne's joys, and the affectionate tranquillity between them that ends the book provide *Sense and Sensibility* with one of its most emphatic personal statements: that strong family affection and sympathy can help to minimise poverty and personal loss. Tradition suggests that there were further links between the sisters, in that the men each of them loved, and hoped to marry, died; like Elinor and Marianne, both sisters lost their loves, but unlike them did not recover them or meet with 'second attachments'. The urgency with which Elinor Dashwood strives to guard her own and her sister's unhappiness from the meddling curiosity of outsiders appears, like much else in the novel that relates to Elinor's emotional trials, to be drawn from painful experience.

Jane Austen characteristically drew the bulk of her material from experience, re-working incidents over and over again, and inventing as little as she could. At the same time she carefully broke up and altered what came to her from real incidents and people, until the source was unrecognisable, or at any rate, impossible to establish beyond doubt. Therefore, although readers might believe they see in the unjustly differentiated fortunes of John Dashwood and his three sisters a reflection of the (doubtless often irritating) difference between the incomes of Edward Knight and his sisters Cassandra and Jane, anything approaching an identification of John and Fanny Dashwood with Mr and Mrs Edward Knight would not be justifiable. Characters such as John Dashwood and Mrs Ferrars, Mr Collins and Lady Catherine de Bourgh in *Pride and Prejudice*, or General Tilney in *Northanger Abbey* are the 'ogres' and 'monsters' in Jane Austen's fiction; they represent qualities (notably greed and hypocrisy) that Jane Austen seems to have disliked and resented very much in their real-life manifestations, for she sets them up in novel after novel to be suitably humbled or defeated by her witty and sensitive heroines. But they derive their distinctive qualities, comic as well as disagreeable, from many sources and not from a single identifiable one.

The turbulence of European politics in her time touched Jane Austen indirectly. Her brothers sent home exciting accounts of their experiences at sea, yet little of this interesting material was drawn upon by her in the writing of her novels except a few minor details, such as the names of ships. Her letters indicate that her actual world was much less limited than the social world she pictures in her novels. The factors governing her rigorous exclusion of certain kinds of material and her equally deliberate selection of other kinds when writing her fiction must be taken into account when her technique is examined and her importance as a novelist is assessed (see Part 3).

Her writing reflects contemporary ideas more than it does contemporary events. 'Sense', for example, is a term that occurs frequently in Jane Austen's novels and letters, and is of great significance in any discussion of her ideas about life. 'Sense' is related to 'reason', the mainstay of eighteenth-century thinking that was elevated to the level of a vice or virtue because man's possession of reasoning power enabled him correctly to understand his own position in the order of natural creation: poised between the animals and the angels, his duty the worship and sober imitation of God. Translated into the terms of ordinary experience, the absence of the attribute of 'sense' or its presence provides the basis upon which the personalities of new acquaintances could be assessed: 'A handsome young man certainly, with quiet, gentlemanlike manners. I set him down as sensible rather than Brilliant', wrote Jane Austen of a person who had been introduced to her. The absence of 'good' or 'common' sense provides the basis for many of her fictional portraits of insincere or pretentious people. 'Sense' and 'reason' extended their range as Jane Austen matured, to include moral virtue as well as social tact and active intelligence. Although *Sense and Sensibility* is the earliest published among her novels, even here 'sense' applies to much more than literature: it becomes the foundation, in the words of Elinor Dashwood, 'on which everything good may be built'.

The article on 'sensibility' in the 1797 edition of the *Encyclopaedia Britannica* gives us an idea of what the term meant in Jane Austen's time:

A nice and delicate perception of pleasure or pain, beauty or deformity. It is very nearly allied to taste; and as far as it is natural seems to depend upon the organisation of the nervous system . . . It is capable . . . of cultivation and is experienced in a much higher degree in civilised than in savage nations, and among persons liberally educated than among boors and illiterate mechanics.

Jane Austen had been preceded in her discussion of 'sensibility' in novels by earlier writers. Laurence Sterne, in both *Tristram Shandy* (1759–67) and *A Sentimental Journey* (1768), had presented 'sensibility' as a positive agent of good, and a way of penetrating to man's inner world of emotions and physical sensations. Mrs Radcliffe, whose novels Jane Austen lightheartedly satirised in *Northanger Abbey*, presented a heroine in *The Mysteries of Udolpho* (1794) whose feelings are both delicate and powerful, and a villain whose horrific career and death illustrate the effects of uncontrolled sensibility. An earlier work, Henry Mackenzie's *The Man of Feeling* (1771), embodied sensibility in a central male character who feels sympathy for, and relieves the distresses of, others. Jane Austen's own approach to the concept of sensibility is shown in her novel to have been appreciative, but cautious. Her criticism is directed at the misuse of sensibility, rather than at sensibility itself; and she views the quality of sense (very much an eighteenth-century virtue, that she values as highly as Pope or Johnson did) as necessarily complementary to sensibility, modifying, controlling, indeed 'civilising' it. In her novel, those who misuse sensibility are seen (though they may be intelligent and sensitive people) to lack sense: Marianne Dashwood and her mother are the main objects of Jane Austen's concern in this regard, and, appropriately satirised, they amend their extreme attitudes in time. But those who misuse sense and lack sensibility are seen as beyond reform, and these are the characters selected for Jane Austen's most withering scorn: John and Fanny Dashwood, Lucy Steele and Robert Ferrars, and Mrs Ferrars.

'Taste' was another favourite topic, and in *Sense and Sensibility* there are numerous characters who either possess trained aesthetic judgement or pretend to have it. The eighteenth century looked for pleasure in what it termed the 'beautiful', the 'picturesque' and the 'sublime', each of which was stated in the writings of aesthetic philosophers to be discoverable in specific natural or man-made phenomena: hence Edward's teasing of Marianne that she would buy 'every book that tells her how to admire an old twisted tree' (Volume I, Chapter 17), and his own sturdy preference for utility ('a snug farmhouse') over the picturesque (Volume I, Chapter 18). Critical terms applied to art, literature and music such as 'elegance', 'propriety', 'simplicity' and 'spirit' are used fastidiously by Jane Austen (and by Elinor and Marianne) in their pure eighteenth-century sense, but certain statements in the novel indicate that ignorance and mere fashionableness were rapidly diluting the effectiveness of such terms. 'Admiration of landscape scenery is become a mere jargon,' complains Marianne (Volume I, Chapter 18), and Lady Middleton describes Elinor and Marianne as 'satirical' without being very sure what the word means (Volume II, Chapter 14). The possession of good 'taste', like the possession and humane use of 'sense' and 'sensibility', becomes a criterion for the assessment of character and intelligence. Marianne's conversations with Edward on 'picturesque' beauty (Volume I, Chapters 17 and 18) and Robert Ferrars's anxiety to be thought an expert on artistic design in matters ranging from toothpick-cases (Volume II, Chapter 11) to cottages (Volume II, Chapter 14) need to be viewed in relation to contemporary ideas regarding (and a widespread respect for) the possessor of a discriminating taste. Jane Austen's handling of her characters' styles of speech and writing (see Part 3) is a particularly interesting aspect of the way her novel reflects contemporary ideas regarding aesthetics and links them to firmly-held moral concepts.

Jane Austen died, after a year of deteriorating health, in 1817 at the age of forty-one. She was buried in Winchester Cathedral.

A note on the text

Jane Austen began writing *Sense and Sensibility* in 1797, when she was twenty-two (a very little senior to her heroine, Elinor Dashwood). It was to be a novel in the form of a series of letters (the epistolary style) after the influential fashion set by Samuel Richardson's novels *Pamela* (1740) and *Clarissa* (1747–48), but in later drafts between 1797 and 1799 Jane Austen abandoned this form and the novel as we know it today presents incident and action almost entirely from a single point of view (that of Elinor Dashwood). After further revision between 1809 and 1810, *Sense and Sensibility* finally appeared in print in 1811. It was the first of her novels to be published, and it was fourteen years in preparation. Jane Austen's characteristic method of writing was to prepare an initial draft, which she would work upon for varied lengths of time afterwards, and subject to a thorough revision before publication. Although all of her novels were published in the last seven years of her life, the first versions of *Northanger Abbey, Pride and Prejudice* and *Sense and Sensibility* were already in draft form when the family moved to Bath in 1800. *Sense and Sensibility* is therefore a novel of her girlhood (although revised in comparative maturity) and the ideas handled in it (the concept of 'sensibility' and the taste for 'picturesque' beauty are examples) are late eighteenth-century ideas. Despite this, the book enjoyed a mild success that encouraged its author to attempt further ventures. *Pride and Prejudice* (begun in 1796, under the title 'First Impressions') was published in 1813, and went into a second edition that year. 'You will be glad to hear that every copy of S&S is sold & that it has brought me £140—besides the copyright, if that shd. ever be of any value,' wrote Jane Austen to her brother Francis in 1813. 'I have now therefore written myself into £250—which only makes me long for more.'

The title-page of *Sense and Sensibility* bore the superscription: 'By a Lady'. *Pride and Prejudice*, when it appeared, was described as being 'By the Author of *Sense and Sensibility*'. No doubt Jane Austen preferred to avoid the publicity authorship might bring her; also, perhaps, she wished her trenchant criticisms of contemporary society to secure general discussion and even influence without being traced back to her. *Mansfield Park* appeared in 1814, and although its author's identity was still unknown (to the general public at least), Jane Austen's authorship was ceasing to be a secret. She published *Emma* in 1815, dedicating it (with royal permission) to the Prince Regent. In 1818 her name appeared for the first time on a title-page, when *Persuasion* was published posthumously; and later in the same year, *Northanger Abbey* appeared. Although her novels, especially *Emma*, were praised by such a respected critic and author as Sir Walter Scott, they were by no means best-sellers. Few of her books reached a second edition in her lifetime, and her collected works published in 1833 was not exhausted until 1882.

Today the position is very different. In 1975 Britain honoured her achievement as a novelist by celebrating the two hundredth anniversary of her birth on a national scale. Every fragment of her writings, poems, skits, scraps of letters, has been carefully edited and preserved for posterity, and her fiction, both published and unpublished, has been the subject of innumerable studies of a scholarly as well as of a light-hearted character. Kipling's story 'The Janeites' signalled Jane Austen's metamorphosis in Victorian times into a cult figure. In our own day it has been written of her by the critic F.R. Leavis that 'she not only makes tradition for those coming after, but ... creates the tradition we see leading down to her. Her work, like the work of all great creative writers, gives a meaning to the past.'

Since *Sense and Sensibility* was written and published as a three-volume novel, and since this fact affects the arrangement of events and incidents in it, volume and chapter references are given throughout this book. Readers using an edition undivided into volumes should note that Volume I consists of twenty-two chapters, and Volumes II and III of fourteen each. They are advised to alter the chapter headings in their copies accordingly.

Part 2

Summaries
of SENSE AND SENSIBILITY

A general summary

While it would be unfair to this lively and often extremely comic novel to state that it has been written to prove a point (as we might say of an essay or a dissertation), its title reveals Jane Austen's interest in the impulses behind people's thoughts and actions. The two central characters, Elinor and Marianne Dashwood, respectively represent 'sense' and 'sensibility'. By contrasting the reason, prudence and caution of Elinor with Marianne's passionate feeling, recklessness and extreme sensitivity (through description as well as through her presentation of their speech and actions), and by involving them in a series of events by which their temperaments are subjected to the demands of ordinary life as it was lived at their level of eighteenth-century English society, Jane Austen establishes her principal theme: that sense should harmonise with sensibility in the ideal human personality, each influencing and moderating the activity of the other.

This is the thread that, with a group of subsidiary themes, binds together a very complicated plot, and unifies a large and very diverse cast of characters. The plot is, briefly, as follows.

The twice-married Mr Henry Dashwood dies, his estate at Norland in Sussex passing to his son by his first wife, Mr John Dashwood. His widow and her three daughters become tenants of Barton Cottage in Devonshire at the invitation of Sir John Middleton, a landowner and a distant relation of Mrs Dashwood. At Barton, Marianne meets, in romantic circumstances, and falls in love with, John Willoughby, an attractive young man who satisfied the yearnings of her sentimental imagination by appearing to share enthusiastically her every thought, opinion and artistic taste. They openly display their affection for each other, but Elinor is troubled by the absence of any formal declaration on either side of an intention to marry. When Willoughby is called suddenly away from Devonshire and the lonely Marianne spends all her time thinking sadly of him (indeed, cultivating the melancholy feelings that are readily stimulated in the person of 'sensibility'), her family assume that the pair are privately engaged to marry. This is, however, not the case. Elinor Dashwood has, meanwhile, herself become attached to Edward Ferrars, a brother of her sister-in-law Fanny Dashwood. She believes Edward loves her in return. But as she has very little money in her own right (her family's fortune now being legally in her brother John's possession and he unwilling to assist them), Elinor is aware that an engagement between Edward and herself would be disapproved of by his mother who expects him to marry well. Since Edward and Elinor have not told one another of their mutual affection, no engagement (not even a secret one) exists between them; and when Lucy Steele, a poor and pretty cousin of Lady Middleton, confides to Elinor that Edward Ferrars is already secretly engaged to marry *her*, Elinor decides to try and dismiss all thoughts of marrying Edward from her own mind.

Volume II begins as the two sisters, reacting characteristically to their disappointments (Elinor behaving with such sensible fortitude that no one suspects her sorrow, Marianne yearning openly for Willoughby's company), go to London as the guests of Mrs Jennings, Lady Middleton's mother. Marianne meets Willoughby again, but only to find that he is about to marry another woman, an heiress. Elinor supports Marianne through the agony of this disappointment and, unhappy as she is herself, bears without defence or explanation her sister's bitter accusations of insensitivity and coldheartedness. However, when the secret of Lucy's engagement to Edward is accidentally disclosed by Lucy's sister Anne to Mrs John Dashwood and the enraged Mrs Ferrars (and freely discussed by everyone else), Marianne recognises for the first time the full extent of both her sister's heroism and her own self-indulgence and selfishness. Both sisters are unhappy at the close of Volume II. But Elinor can draw some consolation from the fact that her sense and prudence have helped her to guard her own privacy and support Marianne through her troubles; while Marianne has little that she can look back on without regret.

Elinor and Marianne leave London to stay with Mr and Mrs Palmer (she is Mrs Jennings's younger daughter) in Somersetshire. Careless and neglectful of her own health, Marianne contracts pneumonia and very nearly dies. Hearing that she is dying, Willoughby rides to Cleveland and interviews Elinor. He tells her of his unhappy marriage, and explains that his own extravagance and selfishness had led him so heavily into debt that he had believed the only course left to him was to give up his affection for Marianne and marry a wealthy woman. When Marianne recovers, the sisters return to Barton. Told by Elinor of Willoughby's confession, Marianne shows that her experiences have taught her good sense; she ascribes her sorrows to their true cause: 'I have nothing to regret—nothing but my own folly.'

The unselfishness and strength of Elinor's character can be seen in the fact that, although she has given up all hope of marrying Edward Ferrars herself, she encourages Colonel Brandon (a friend, met originally at Barton, where he became a distant but very sincere admirer of Marianne) in his decision to present Edward with a living on his estate at

Delaford. This will, Elinor believes, enable Edward to follow his own inclination to take orders and marry Lucy, thus putting an end to his dependence on his mother. She now daily expects news of Edward's marriage to Lucy. It comes, reported by a servant, and Elinor resigns herself to what she has long regarded as inevitable: her own unhappiness and loneliness. But correction is at hand. Edward himself comes to Barton, to tell the Dashwoods that Lucy has broken their engagement and married his younger brother Robert (who now owns the property Edward lost when their mother, enraged by the news of his engagement to Lucy, disinherited him). Edward explains the true nature of his earlier entanglement with Lucy, asks Elinor to marry him, and is accepted. Their marriage is necessarily delayed, for to marry on an inadequate income would be an act of foolish 'sensibility' rather than of prudent 'sense'. But in time Mrs Ferrars is reconciled with Edward, and provides him with financial assistance. Edward and Elinor move to their new home at Delaford Parsonage on Colonel Brandon's estate, and after a lapse of time Marianne recovers sufficiently from her disappointment over Willoughby to allow herself a second attachment. She becomes the wife of Colonel Brandon, and the two sisters maintain the affection that has linked them in all the experiences described in the novel.

It will be noticed from the summary above that two other characters support and reinforce the virtues of sense and sensibility: Edward Ferrars, whose sense of honour guides him throughout his burdensome relationship with Lucy Steele; and Colonel Brandon, whose generous sympathy for others is translated into positive and helpful action on their behalf. In the chapter-by-chapter synopses that follow, the reader will be able to perceive how certain additional (but comparatively minor) personalities are introduced to interact with the four major characters. It should be noted at the same time that certain minor incidents and details have been omitted in the general summary above, in order to convey an idea of the way Jane Austen develops her theme by means of the major events and incidents in her story: each significant event is a turning-point, or a new stage in the process by which Marianne and Elinor learn more about life and discipline themselves. In the chapter-by-chapter synopses the reader will be able to appreciate Jane Austen's skill in introducing subsidiary events that are in the nature of 'sub-plots' and interweave with happenings in the main plot.

One example of a minor character who figures in just such a 'sub-plot' is Eliza Williams, Colonel Brandon's ward. Willoughby seduces her, and the two gentlemen fight a duel on her account according to the custom of the time. Since it is the knowledge of Willoughby's connection with Eliza that, coming to the ears of his wealthy kinswoman Mrs Smith, causes his hasty departure from Devonshire, the existence of this character temporarily ruins Marianne's happiness and brings about the first stage in her progress towards a more sensible outlook upon life. Yet she remains a minor character in the novel, since we never see her nor do we hear her speak, and the history both of the duel and of her mother's experiences is only related by Colonel Brandon to Elinor and not presented in action.

Detailed summaries

Volume I Chapter 1

Two deaths, following close upon one another, cause Mrs Henry Dashwood and her three daughters to descend rapidly from wealth to very reduced circumstances. Despite the fact that his father had, on his deathbed, urged him to look after the step-mother and sisters whose wealth he soon will legally inherit, Mr John Dashwood (encouraged by his equally cold-hearted and selfish wife Fanny) takes immediate possession of Norland Park. The sensitive, emotional temperament of Mrs Henry Dashwood and the similar, yet contrasting personalities of Elinor and Marianne reveal themselves through these characters' several reactions to this trying situation, and also in their respective ways of mourning Mr Henry Dashwood's death.

NOTES AND GLOSSARY:

moiety: half
tardy: late, slow
fortune: dowry; wealth bestowed on a woman at the time of her marriage
not merely from interest: not merely from a care for their own profit or advancement
an imperfect articulation: a lisp
sanguine: hopeful, courageous
rendered easy: made comfortable
propriety: correct behaviour
indelicacy: insensitivity; disregard for others' feelings
romance: fancifulness; tendency to prefer the elements of romantic and imaginative fiction to the plainness of everyday life

Volume I Chapter 2

This chapter provides a further brief sketch of Mrs Henry Dashwood's character that emphasises her likeness to Marianne. The rest of this very famous chapter is devoted to a dialogue between John and Fanny

Dashwood as they consider how best they can avoid fulfilling their obligations to Mrs Henry Dashwood and her daughters. A reference by Fanny to her mother's annoyance at having to pay annuities to three aged family retainers by the terms of her father's will serves to link Fanny with her mother in selfishness, as Marianne and Mrs Dashwood have (at the start of the chapter) been linked in 'sensibility'

NOTES AND GLOSSARY:

eligible: suitable
alloy: moderation
conceive: imagine
temper: temperament
light-headed: delirious; not in his right mind
annuity: the grant of an annual sum for life
indecorous: unseemly, incorrect behaviour
plate: silver-plated utensils for household use, for example cutlery for the table, serving dishes
amazing: colloquial version of 'very'
how excessively comfortable: Fanny's uncertain grammar betrays her lack of refinement in matters more important than the use of language

---

Volume I Chapter 3

Edward Ferrars's character is sketched in negative terms: by describing him as 'not handsome' and 'diffident' (shy), and by presenting Marianne's criticism of his lacking 'grace' of figure, 'spirit' and 'fire' of expression, and 'real taste', Jane Austen indirectly challenges the popular novel of sensibility and sentiment, in which heroes were invariably presented in the exaggerated terms used by Marianne. A contrast is effected between two families: Marianne and Mrs Dashwood like Edward for his personal qualities and because of his obvious affection for Elinor, but Mrs Ferrars and her daughter Fanny care nothing for such qualities and only want Edward to distinguish himself in political or fashionable life. Marianne's remarks to her sympathetic mother about Edward should be carefully noted. The rhythm of her speech mirrors her emotional, enthusiastic nature (see her description of Edward reading aloud from the poetry of Cowper), and her opinions on love and marriage arise more from idealism and fancy than from common sense. Such ideas as hers, while obviously similar to those acted upon by heroines in novels of sensibility, are natural to youth (she is only seventeen years old), but the passion with which she expresses them prepares the reader for further interesting revelations regarding such a stormy personality.

NOTES AND GLOSSARY:

doctrine: belief
address: conversational manner
barouche: a four-wheeled carriage
trifling: not worth serious consideration
Fortunately he had a younger brother who was more promising: an example of Jane Austen's characteristic irony. The statement appears as a comment by the narrator, but represents the trivial point of view adopted by Mrs Ferrars. The reader would conclude, not that Edward is to be despised for his quiet tastes, but that he is a much worthier and more interesting person than his younger brother
taste: appreciation of the beautiful in nature or art
sensibility: readiness to be emotionally moved (by the pathetic in art or literature)

Volume I Chapter 4

Elinor and Marianne discuss Edward Ferrars, first as a man of 'taste' and then as a personality. Marianne believes a man of taste cannot fail to be also a man of virtue, but Elinor's ideas are much more down-to-earth. The sisters differ, not only in their ideas about aesthetic taste and the opposite sex, but also in their ideas about the nature and expression of love. Elinor confesses her high 'esteem' for Edward, but sensibly will not allow herself to think too hopefully of marrying him, since she is aware of his financial dependence on his mother and judges that Mrs Ferrars will not favour his marriage to a girl without money or high rank. She is proved right in this, for Fanny Dashwood perceives the growing affection between Edward and Elinor and makes it insultingly clear to Mrs Henry Dashwood that a marriage between them would not be tolerated by her mother. Mrs Dashwood cannot bear to expose Elinor any longer to such treatment, and wishes to leave Norland immediately. A letter from a kinsman, Sir John Middleton, offering her the tenancy of a small house on his Devonshire property, now arrives and the offer is accepted by Mrs Dashwood. Although privately reluctant to travel so far from Edward, Elinor sees the wisdom of moving away from her brother's family and (since they are no longer well off) of taking a house that can be economically run. Her quiet agreement to her mother's plan further demonstrates how sense guides and controls the deep feeling that is in her nature.

NOTES AND GLOSSARY:

propensities: qualities

engrossed:	occupied
sentiments:	opinions
just:	exact, accurate
conjectured:	fancied
esteem:	respect
partiality:	liking
amiable:	goodnatured
felicity:	happiness
regard:	feeling, attitude
genius:	talent, natural inclination
indifference:	impartiality; showing neither like nor dislike
aggrandisement:	spectacular advancement
draw him in:	entangle him (in an unsuitable love affair)

Volume I Chapter 5

Mrs Henry Dashwood agrees to rent Barton Cottage for a year, and makes rapid preparations to leave Norland. John Dashwood offers no financial help, and Fanny shows thinly-disguised satisfaction at their going. Edward is disturbed to hear that they will be so far away, and is invited by Mrs Dashwood to visit them at Barton. All the Dashwood girls are saddened by the thought of leaving their old home, but Marianne's solitary soliloquy addressed to the trees in the park underlines what Jane Austen has called in a previous chapter the 'excess of her sensibility'.

NOTES AND GLOSSARY:
incommode:	inconvenience
give over:	abandon

determine her future household: decide how many servants she would employ, and whether or not she would maintain horses and a carriage for the use (and consequence) of the family

Volume I Chapter 6

The Dashwood family meet their landlord. Sir John Middleton (unlike John Dashwood) shows every concern for them, although his generous kindness is a little marred by the persistence with which he forces it on others. Lady Middleton is handsome and well-bred, but reserved and unoriginal in her conversation. The Dashwoods find the house comfortable but they do not think the Middletons particularly good company, although they appreciate Sir John's kindness.

NOTES AND GLOSSARY:

as a cottage it was defective: Jane Austen is gently satirising romantic tastes that preferred thatched roofs and honeysuckle on the walls (despite the inconvenience of damp!) to the comforts of an ordinary tiled house. See *Northanger Abbey*, where Catherine Morland is disappointed to find a comfortable modern house where she had hoped for a ruined Gothic monastery

waiting on Mrs Dashwood: paying Mrs Dashwood a formal visit

On every formal visit a child ought to be of the party: an ironic comment by the author that indicates how meaningless and dull such occasions often were, since the people present had been brought together by mere rules of etiquette and not by common interests or affection

---

Volume I Chapter 7

The Dashwoods call on the Middletons. A satiric description of the Middletons' way of life. Two new characters are introduced, Mrs Jennings and Colonel Brandon. Marianne is asked to play the piano, and the Colonel recommends himself to the Dashwoods (and even to romantic Marianne) by being the only person present to listen with attentiveness and appreciation.

NOTES AND GLOSSARY:

piqued herself: prided herself

unaffected: simple, natural. While Sir John is right in thinking his nieces devoid of pretentiousness, he underestimates them in considering them 'simple'!

within his own manor: like other landowners of the time, Sir John maintains game birds on his property, and would not have welcomed the presence of another sportsman equally interested in regular shooting

vulgar: lacking refinement in manners and conversation

insipidity: dullness, lifelessness

giving up music: a satiric hint that Lady Middleton, like many of her contemporaries, had learned to play the piano as a qualification for marriage, rather than from any love of music

---

Volume I Chapter 8

Marianne's views on men and marriage are further developed in a discussion (*a*) of Colonel Brandon, who Mrs Jennings has suggested is in love with her, and (*b*) of Edward, who she thinks lacks the passionate urgency she would expect in a lover. Marianne considers 35-year-old Colonel Brandon altogether too old, sick and dull for marriage, except with some ageing spinster who might accept him out of charity, desperation, or a need for security. The 'strange' composure displayed towards each other by Edward and Elinor disappoints Marianne.

NOTES AND GLOSSARY:

jointure: legal arrangement by which a widow holds property in her own right on the death of her husband
projecting: planning, speculating

Volume I Chapter 9

Marianne sprains her ankle during a walk on the downs and is rescued by a handsome and personable stranger, Mr John Willoughby. Sir John informs the Dashwoods that Willoughby is the future owner of nearby Allenham Court, and owns an estate of his own in Somersetshire. The Dashwoods all think him interesting and attractive, and Marianne believes she has at last discovered a man who accords with her idea of a hero in romantic fiction.

NOTES AND GLOSSARY:

chagrined: disappointed
pointers: hunting dogs
to make himself still more interesting: a sly hint from the author that the romantic circumstances of a rescue and a storm have helped Willoughby to make a good impression
gallantry: courtesy, chivalry
crimsoned over her face: blush
becoming: graces the wearer
intelligence: information, news

Volume I Chapter 10

Willoughby becomes a frequent visitor at the Cottage, and it is soon clear that he and Marianne have a good deal in common and have fallen in love. Elinor finds, with pity, that Mrs Jennings has been right in believing Colonel Brandon in love with Marianne. She thinks him most unlikely to succeed in competition with the witty and lively Willoughby, and is alone in defending his character when Marianne and Willoughby exercise their wit at the Colonel's expense. Elinor likes Willoughby, but fears that he (like Marianne) tends to be too self-indulgent, hasty in his judgement, and too individualistic for his own good.

NOTES AND GLOSSARY:

decorum: correct behaviour
raillery: teasing
peculiarly: especially
ardour: energetic enthusiasm
in the mass: generalised
elegance: flourish, style. Note the different use of the same word in Chapter 3. Later in this paragraph, Jane Austen refers to the 'elegance ... of the family': here the meaning is once again that of neatness and orderliness
every matter of importance: poetry is more important to Marianne than most other things, suggests Elinor teasingly
Cowper and Scott; Pope: William Cowper (1731–1800) and Sir Walter Scott (1771–1832), being popular romantic poets who wrote of passionate human feelings and wild, romantic landscapes, are among Marianne's favourites. Alexander Pope (1688–1744), then falling out of fashion, and moreover an urban poet, who chose 'correctness' as his aim, is less admired by her
picturesque beauty: that type of natural beauty (generally of landscape) that was regarded as fit to be the subject of an effective picture

Volume I Chapter 11

Marianne and Willoughby publicly display their liking for each other to Elinor's private (but only tactfully-voiced) concern. Colonel Brandon discusses Marianne's romantic prejudice against second attachments with Elinor, who is left with the conviction that Marianne reminds him of a former and unhappy love affair

NOTES AND GLOSSARY:

serious employment: reading, study, sewing, music, painting (and possibly gardening) would occupy the time of the Dashwood sisters. None of them would, according to the conventions of the time and their social class, have worked (that is, been 'employed') for a living
minutia: details

Volume I Chapter 12

Willoughby plans to give Marianne a horse as a present. Elinor's suggestion that acceptance of such an expensive gift from such a recent acquaintance would be improper is scornfully rejected by Marianne, who cannot tolerate formality. Elinor successfully persuades her to refuse the gift by reminding her that maintenance of the horse would inevitably cost their mother a great deal of money. From Willoughby's remarks on learning that his gift must be refused, Elinor deduces that he and Marianne are privately engaged to marry each other. Margaret's news that Marianne has given Willoughby a lock of her hair as a keepsake seems to be a further confirmation. Margaret tactlessly reveals to Mrs Jennings that Elinor has a 'favourite', who lives at Norland and whose name begins with an 'F'. The Middletons plan an excursion to Whitwell for the following day.

NOTES AND GLOSSARY:

intimacy: close acquaintance

tender: sensitive

a lock of her hair: not a present to be lightly given, since it is so personal as to indicate an intimate relationship. See Pope's poem, *The Rape of the Lock* (1712, 1714), in which a dandy steals a lock of hair from a society beauty, causing a bitter quarrel between their respective families

to see a very fine place: wealthy landowners of the time were fond of employing landscape gardeners to 'improve' the beauty of their grounds. The 'noble piece of water' is very likely to have been an artificial lake, introduced to create a picturesque effect and please the artistic taste of the owner and his visitors

Volume I Chapter 13

The excursion to Whitwell has to be postponed, for Colonel Brandon (whose presence is essential to the party's gaining admittance to the grounds) is called away to London on urgent and mysterious 'business'. Gossip-loving Mrs Jennings tells Elinor she is sure the 'business' concerns a Miss Williams, the Colonel's 'natural' (illegitimate) daughter. She also makes it her business to find out where Willoughby and Marianne spend the morning, and challenges them to deny that they have been visiting Allenham Court, at present occupied by his elderly and infirm aunt, Mrs Smith. Elinor cannot believe Marianne would have acted so indiscreetly as to pay such a visit uninvited and un-chaperoned, but on inquiry is told quite frankly by Marianne that the story is perfectly true. Marianne is quite sure her action has not been wrong, and declares she never spent a more pleasant morning in her life.

NOTES AND GLOSSARY:

changed colour: bad news has possibly made the Colonel grow pale

lay fifty guineas: bet or wager this amount

go post: travel with relays of horses. His proposed method of travel indicates the Colonel's intention to lose no time

Miss Dashwood: Elinor, as the eldest in the family, would be addressed as 'Miss Dashwood'. Her younger sisters would be addressed as 'Miss Marianne' and 'Miss Margaret'

natural daughter: a daughter born out of wedlock, that is, her mother would not be the Colonel's legal wife. Mrs Jennings's lack of refinement may be seen in the way she mentions this matter to Elinor, who is herself unmarried and only nineteen years old

happiness could only be enjoyed: satiric humour at the expense of Sir John Middleton, who can take no pleasure in solitude or quietness

I am not sensible: I am not aware, or conscious

Volume I Chapter 14

Elinor is distressed by the failure of Willoughby and Marianne to announce the engagement that their behaviour suggests must exist. Willoughby says that any alteration to Barton Cottage would wound him: it is clear that the inconvenient little house is dear to him because in it he has come to know Marianne.

NOTES AND GLOSSARY:

involved: financially encumbered, burdened

prescience: foreknowledge; a mysterious prompting

Volume I Chapter 15

Willoughby informs an astonished Dashwood family that Mrs Smith wishes him to leave immediately on business to London. Asked by Mrs Dashwood to return to Barton Cottage as a guest when his business is completed, Willoughby cannot even promise that, and leaves in great haste, to Marianne's distress and Elinor's unwilling but unconquerable suspicion that he is treating them (and particularly Marianne) less honourably and frankly than they would have expected of him. Mrs Dashwood, who is very fond of Willoughby, theorises and speculates in his favour, but Elinor (though hopeful that she may be right) cannot share her confidence in him. Marianne's sorrow distresses them all.

NOTES AND GLOSSARY:
exhilaration: being cheered
ungracious: unkind, uncharitable
illiberal a foundation: unfair basis
fortitude: strength of mind

Volume I Chapter 16

Marianne's sensibility is fully displayed in the violence with which she mourns Willoughby's absence. As time passes and no letter from him appears, Elinor asks her mother to question Marianne as to whether an engagement exists between them or not; but Mrs Dashwood, full of 'romantic delicacy' and concern for Marianne, refuses to do so. Edward Ferrars visits Barton Cottage. His manner to Elinor seems disappointingly cold, but she behaves with characteristic good sense and treats him with the respect due to a brother-in-law.

NOTES AND GLOSSARY:
Her sensibility was potent enough!: there could be no doubt about the power of her capacity for emotion
indulgence of feeling: giving emotion free play
romantic delicacy: an unwillingness to offend that goes beyond the requirements of good sense
nice: fastidious
dirty: muddy

Volume I Chapter 17

A chapter of conversation. Edward's reserve relaxes somewhat under Mrs Dashwood's warm welcome, but he is plainly not his usual self. The conversation exposes further points of difference between Elinor's sense and Marianne's sensibility.

NOTES AND GLOSSARY:
with no inclination for expense: Mrs Dashwood ironically states her contempt for the ostentatious tastes of people who hanker for public notoriety
hunters: horses suitable for the sport of riding to hounds
Thomson: James Thomson (1700–48), who wrote *The Seasons* (1726–30) which describes natural scenery
how to admire an old twisted tree: Edward teases Marianne about her passion for the picturesque
expressively: meaningfully

Volume I Chapter 18

Edward's opinion of a pleasing landscape disappoints romantic Marianne. Edward is seen to wear a ring containing a lock of hair he says is his sister Fanny's, but which Elinor suspects to be her own. Mrs Jennings identifies Edward as Elinor's unknown lover at Norland whose name begins with an 'F'.

NOTES AND GLOSSARY:

utility: practical usefulness
jargon: cant
hackneyed: rendered trite and commonplace
banditti: Italian outlaws, often introduced as heroic and picturesque characters in the popular novels of the time

Volume I Chapter 19

Edward leaves Barton Cottage. Elinor excuses his unusually abrupt behaviour more easily than she did Willoughby's a short time before. Her self-control is most unlike Marianne's deliberate self-indulgence, but it is clear to the reader that she feels as deeply. The Middletons call at the cottage with their relations, Mr and Mrs Palmer.

NOTES AND GLOSSARY:

candid: frank
nicety: fastidiousness
temporising: humouring; letting her have her own way for the time
genteel: gentlemanly
augment: increase
a red coat: an army uniform
less abstruse: more easily understood
prepossessing: pleasing
entered at Oxford: admitted to Oxford University as an undergraduate
Columella: Lucius Junius Moderatus Columella, a Roman of the first century AD, born in Spain, who in the course of his life became a soldier, a tribune, a farmer, a poet, and a writer on agricultural subjects. While farming in Italy, he wrote *De arboribus* ('On trees') and the *De re rustica* ('On rural matters') in twelve books, the tenth of which was written as a supplement to the *Georgics* of Virgil

Volume I Chapter 20

Some light relief is introduced, in a chapter devoted to the Palmers

NOTES AND GLOSSARY:

chaperon: escort
droll: amusing
an MP: a Member of Parliament
frank for me: lend his signature, so that my letters may be carried post-free. Members of Parliament still enjoyed this privilege in the early nineteenth century
monstrous: very; Mrs Palmer, Fanny Dashwood, Mrs Jennings, Sir John Middleton and the Steeles are all distinguished from Elinor and Marianne by their use of slang

Volume I Chapter 21

Anne and Lucy Steele arrive as guests at Barton Park, and please Lady Middleton by flattering her and humouring her children. Sir John Middleton gossips to the Steeles about Elinor's suspected attachment to Edward Ferrars. The Steeles awaken Elinor's curiosity by stating that they know Edward well.

NOTES AND GLOSSARY:

gave way: could not compete
tolerable gentility: passably well-born and good-mannered
benevolent man!: satire at the expense of people such as Sir John Middleton, who are indiscriminate in their friendships
some kind of sense: the Steeles have the intelligence to realise that flattering Lady Middleton will profit them; but theirs is far from being the 'sense' Elinor represents in the novel
swallow anything: believe anything
telling lies when politeness required it: one of the trying demands society makes upon individuals. Marianne's proud individualism forbids such deceits as Elinor, though inwardly as honest and critical as her sister, finds she must practise for the sake of politeness
prodigious: very
smart beaux: male admirers, dandies
vast addition: an asset
as lief: equally, just as much

Volume I Chapter 22

Lucy Steele informs Elinor that she has been engaged to Edward for four years, and shows her Edward's portrait and a letter she has received from him. She also tells her that Edward wears a lock of her (Lucy's) hair in a ring, and that he had spent a fortnight with her family at Plymouth before journeying on to stay with the Dashwoods in Devonshire. Elinor cannot doubt the truth of Lucy's statements. She does not give way to her shocked and distressed feelings, however, until Lucy has left and she is alone.

NOTES AND GLOSSARY:

rectitude: high principles, honesty
integrity of mind: soundness, sincerity of mind
divine: work out, imagine
incredulity: unbelief
quite as his own sisters: Lucy is making it clear to Elinor that Edward regards her merely with the affection due to a sister, and not a future wife
miniature: a portrait painted on ivory, on a very small scale
Your own judgement must direct you: Elinor does not take advantage of the situation to suggest that Lucy should indeed break off her engagement to Edward
veracity: truthfulness
mortified: humiliated
wretched: miserable
confounded: defeated
You know his hand: You are familiar with his handwriting

(Volume I ends with Chapter 22 in the third and subsequent editions)

Volume II Chapter 1

Elinor wishes to convince Lucy that she has not been hurt by the news of her engagement to Edward, and while on a visit to the Park manages to engage Lucy in conversation while Marianne's piano-playing prevents their being overheard by the other ladies in the room: an early example of Jane Austen's skill in using the details of everyday life (here the making of a filigree basket for a spoiled child) to good purpose in furthering her artistic intentions.

NOTES AND GLOSSARY:

dupe: victim, one who has been fooled
poignant: sharp

alacrity: readiness

Lady Middleton was happily preserved: satiric fun at the expense of persons who are bored by their own company

fillagree: jewel work of a delicate kind made with threads and beads, usually of gold or silver. The making of filigree ornaments and baskets (like embroidery, the netting of purses and the making of artificial flowers) were favourite pursuits among young ladies of leisure

a rubber of Casino: a game of cards

a little of that address: a little of that (dutiful) courtesy

gained her own end: got what she wanted

wrapt up: absorbed

Volume II Chapter 2

Lucy tells Elinor that her fear of Mrs Ferrars's displeasure (which might cause the disinheritance of Edward in favour of his younger brother Robert) prevents the announcement of their engagement. She asks Elinor to persuade John Dashwood to present Edward with the living at Norland when he has taken orders (since he wishes to become a clergyman). By the end of their interview Elinor is convinced that Edward has wearied of his engagement to Lucy, but is prevented by his sense of duty from ending it; and that Lucy no longer cares for him, but is unwilling to let the chance (slim though it is) of marrying a wealthy man slip away from her.

NOTES AND GLOSSARY:

breaking the ice: making the first move

disinterestedness: lack of bias; impartiality

coxcomb: conceited person, a fop

he would prefer the church: 'taking orders' as a clergyman was regarded as being almost as much a profession as enlisting in the Army or Navy, standing for Parliament, or enrolling as a barrister in the courts of law

your interest: a good word in his favour from you. Promotions in all professions came most easily and rapidly to men who had powerful connections, and did not hesitate to make use of them

Norland living: the position of Vicar or principal clergyman of Norland. Such a benefice or 'living' was John Dashwood's to award to a candidate of his choice. Later in the novel, Colonel Brandon gives Edward the Delaford living

a very good one:	certain privileges and property (including the Vicarage itself) accompanied the grant of a living. Lucy is referring to these material benefits, not to the high spiritual state of Norland's parishioners
confidante:	intimate friend (an ironic use of the word, for Elinor and Lucy dislike each other heartily). A heroine's confidante was often a minor character of importance in contemporary fiction
that festival:	an ironic reference to the ostentatious manner in which people of wealth celebrated Christmas

Volume II Chapter 3

Mrs Jennings invites Elinor and Marianne to spend the winter season in London, as her guests. Marianne is eager, Elinor reluctant, to go. After much debate the invitation is accepted.

NOTES AND GLOSSARY:

improved:	better informed, more accomplished
condition in life:	social rank
a less elegant part of the town:	a less fashionable area
traded with success:	businessmen's families were regarded as being several degrees less genteel than those of gentlemen; there is a clear distinction of social rank implied in the reference to the late Mr Jennings as a trader
laugh at my odd ways:	Mrs Jennings seems to be more perceptive than Elinor and Marianne have given her credit for being!
perturbation:	excitement
they had never been so happy in their lives:	Jane Austen expresses this (obviously false and insincere) remark in the gushing language habitually used by Anne and Lucy Steele

Volume II Chapter 4

On arriving in London, Marianne writes to Willoughby, but the observant Elinor notes that she receives no answering letter or personal call. Marianne's barely suppressed emotions of feverish expectation and disappointment make her uncongenial company for Mrs Jennings's callers, among them Mrs Palmer and Colonel Brandon

NOTES AND GLOSSARY:

constancy:	faithfulness

fatigue:	weariness
direction:	address
prospect:	future
a happy specimen:	a good example; Jane Austen's use of the word 'happy' here is ironic, for no pleasure can be expected from Marianne's future behaviour if this is a sample of it
a landscape in coloured silks:	an embroidered picture, a sample of the 'accomplishments' young ladies were expected to acquire during the years of their education
a fine size:	an allusion to Mrs Palmer's pregnancy, typical of Mrs Jennings's unrefined way of speaking; the Colonel's reply indicates, by its difference, his superior mind and manners
Bond Street:	a London street, still famous today for its fashionable shops

Volume II Chapter 5

Marianne finds excuses for Willoughby's failure to visit her, or write. She is further disturbed by learning that he is, apparently, deliberately avoiding a meeting with them. Colonel Brandon tells Elinor that Marianne's engagement to Willoughby is 'very generally known', and sadly informs her of his own love for Marianne.

NOTES AND GLOSSARY:

open weather:	fine weather
expedient:	method
she had never dropped:	she had never ceased to treat as her friends; Mrs Jennings's loyalty to her friends is another point in her favour with the reader, although Lady Middleton disapproves of it
his card:	people of fashion carried specially printed or engraved visiting-cards which they left at the homes of their friends if, when a visit was paid, the friends in question were not at home

Volume II Chapter 6

Elinor and Marianne accompany Lady Middleton to a fashionable party, where they encounter Willoughby in the company of an elegantly-dressed young woman. Marianne is surprised and distressed by his obvious reluctance to either speak to her, or acknowledge a close acquaintance. Elinor and Marianne leave the party early.

NOTES AND GLOSSARY:

lavender water: a restorative; ladies carried small bottles of smelling-salts or herb-scented water, to help them recover from the effects of heat or emotion

sporting with (her) affections: paying attentions to her without serious intentions of marriage

Volume II Chapter 7

Next morning Willoughby returns Marianne's letters and the lock of hair she had given him at Barton. In his reply to her reproaches he insolently denies by letter that he had ever given her reason to think he loved her, and announces his imminent marriage to another woman. Elinor finds that no engagement had in fact existed between Marianne and Willoughby. She enters sympathetically into Marianne's sorrow at Willoughby's desertion of her, but feels privately that her sister has escaped a disastrous marriage with an unprincipled and dishonest man.

NOTES AND GLOSSARY:

tremour: trembling

chariot: carriage

persuasion: a belief

scarcely less violent: Elinor's feelings are as intense as Marianne's

this engagement is fulfilled: Willoughby here informs Marianne that he is about to marry another woman

such language: since Willoughby's relationship with the Dashwoods had been so close and Marianne's letters to him so warmly and spontaneously written, the formality of his letter implies a calculated insult

Happy, happy Elinor: Marianne mistakenly believes Elinor's composed manner to spring from her loving confidence in Edward's affection for her

Volume II Chapter 8

Mrs Jennings informs Elinor that Willoughby's extravagance has made him very nearly penniless, and that he is to marry an heiress (Miss Grey) with a fortune of £50,000. She showers well-meant (but not very sensible) kindnesses upon Marianne, who only wants to be left alone. Colonel Brandon tells Elinor that Willoughby's marriage is expected to take place in a few weeks' time.

NOTES AND GLOSSARY:

she is of age: legally entitled to her rights and property as an adult

love-child:	Colonel Brandon's supposed illegitimate daughter (see Volume I, Chapter 13)
stewponds:	ponds or tanks in which fish were kept until needed for the table
unfathomable:	impossible to understand or predict

Volume II Chapter 9

Mrs Jennings's clumsy kindnesses irritate Marianne, who wants to leave London immediately for Barton. Colonel Brandon tells Elinor the history of Eliza Williams, the illegitimate daughter of his dead sister-in-law and former sweetheart, Elizabeth Brandon. Eliza has been seduced and deserted by Willoughby, with whom the Colonel (as her guardian) has fought a duel to avenge her honour. He hopes that hearing the story from Elinor might help Marianne recover more easily from her disappointment, since she might begin to consider herself lucky to have escaped Eliza's fate, and even (because of the likeness of her character to Elizabeth Brandon's) her mother's.

NOTES AND GLOSSARY:

diffuse:	use more words than strictly necessary
seducer:	one who leads another astray, for example, from the duties of a wife
spunging-house:	a place of preliminary confinement for debtors
consumption:	a wasting disease
guilty connection:	extra-marital affair or liaison
she was gone:	she had eloped; there is a similar turn of events in both the novels Jane Austen published after *Sense and Sensibility*: in *Pride and Prejudice* Lydia Bennet elopes from Brighton with George Wickham, and in *Mansfield Park* Maria Rushworth elopes with Henry Crawford
expensive:	extravagant
dissipated:	frivolous, dissolute
we met by appointment:	duels were fought secretly, by appointment, the arrangements regarding time, place, weapons, and so on being made through chosen friends (known as 'seconds') of the two men involved

Volume II Chapter 10

Mrs Dashwood advises her daughters to stay on in London. Elinor manages to restrain Sir John and Mrs Jennings from mentioning Willoughby's name or expressing concern for Marianne in her sister's presence. Willoughby marries, and leaves London with his bride. Anne and Lucy Steele arrive in London.

NOTES AND GLOSSARY:

character: good name, honourable reputation

that visit at Allenham: it is expected that Willoughby will bring his bride to call on Mrs Smith at Allenham

the indignation of them all: an interesting satiric exposure follows, in which the several reactions of different people to Willoughby's behaviour are contrasted. Colonel Brandon's nature emerges, by contrast, as much finer and more sensitive than those of Mrs Jennings's daughters

to have went away: Lucy's characteristically ungrammatical speech

---

Volume II Chapter 11

Elinor and Marianne visit a jeweller's shop. There (though they do not identify him) they witness the stupidly conceited behaviour of Edward's younger brother, Robert Ferrars, and meet their own brother John Dashwood. There follows a severe exposure of John Dashwood's mercenary character, through his speeches and behaviour to Elinor, and the squalid opinions he expresses to her of Marianne, Mrs Jennings, Colonel Brandon and the Middletons. He informs Elinor that Edward's mother plans to match him with an heiress, Miss Morton.

NOTES AND GLOSSARY:

correctness of his eye: exactness of his judgement; this would normally be a statement complimentary to Robert Ferrars's good taste, but the triviality of the object involved (a mere toothpick-case!) indicates that the unknown young man is a fool and a dandy

vouchsafe: yield

settling: marrying

strong natural, sterling insignificance: the impressive climax on the dismissive word '*in*significance', and its combination with the word 'sterling' (usually used of the purest silver, and especially appropriate here since the scene is set in a jeweller's shop) are examples of Jane Austen's early satiric style

But so it ought to be: John Dashwood apparently feels it only proper that the Middletons should show his sisters kindness that he and Fanny (though nearer relations) had neglected to pay!

a most valuable woman: John Dashwood's opinion of Mrs Jennings's 'value' as a friend is based entirely on his estimate of her income

the bloom: the fresh glow on the skin of a newly-ripened fruit; John Dashwood sounds like a grocer pricing the fruit in his shop-window as he assesses the likely price his sister Marianne will fetch in marriage

Volume II Chapter 12

Mr and Mrs John Dashwood invite the Middletons to dinner. Also invited are Mrs Jennings, Elinor and Marianne, Colonel Brandon, and the Steele sisters. Mrs Ferrars is to be present, and Lucy and Elinor look forward (Lucy with trepidation, Elinor with curiosity) to meeting Edward's mother. Wishing to humiliate Elinor, whose suspected relationship with Edward they wish to discourage, Fanny Dashwood and her mother are particularly agreeable to Lucy (of whose secret engagement to Edward they, of course, know nothing).

NOTES AND GLOSSARY:

the quarter of an hour bestowed: the minimum (and according to some, the proper) time required for a social call was fifteen minutes

sedulously: persistently

indigence: poverty

officiously: unduly forward in offering assistance

connoisseurship: knowledge of the fine arts

considerately informing her: warning her

philippic: speech intended to crush any opposition; after the famous 'Philippics' of Cicero (Roman orator and statesman 106–43BC), fourteen speeches in which he supported Octavian and denounced Mark Antony

bustle: fuss, confusion

Volume II Chapter 13

An amusing chapter, in which Lucy calls on Elinor to tell her how happy Mrs Ferrars's condescension the previous evening has made her. Her visit is interrupted by Edward, who has come to call on Elinor and Marianne. Elinor greets him with her usual composure and charming politeness, Marianne with real delight. Lucy goes away very irritated.

NOTES AND GLOSSARY:

affability: pleasantness

hauteur: haughty, proud behaviour

a formal curtsy: a feminine movement of greeting or respect, made by bending the knees slightly and lowering the body; in Lucy's description of behaviour that would have hurt her feelings, she pointedly reminds Elinor of Mrs Ferrars's formal, indeed hostile, behaviour to her

the handsomest manner: the most generous way; by taking her time in calling Marianne, Elinor generously gives Edward and Lucy an opportunity of talking privately

admirable discretion: great tact; ironically intended, as in 'a happy specimen' (see Volume II, Chapter 4)

engaged elsewhere: had an appointment somewhere else

little as well as great: Lucy viciously alludes to Willoughby's recent breaking of his supposed engagement to Marianne

scrupulous: fastidiously careful

Volume II Chapter 14

By a series of circumstances arising from the social meetings of the Middletons, Dashwoods, Steeles and Palmers, Anne and Lucy Steele are invited to stay as guests of John and Fanny Dashwood in their house at Harley Street. Lucy and Elinor (unaware that the invitation has been given so that Fanny Dashwood may escape the obligation of having Elinor and Marianne to stay) feel that the invitation is a sign of even greater kindnesses to come, and Elinor teaches herself to expect the announcement of an engagement between Edward and Lucy as imminent. Robert Ferrars proves himself a fop and a fool in a conversation with Elinor regarding his elder brother Edward, and the attractions of country cottages.

NOTES AND GLOSSARY:

satirical: inclined to be critically aware of the ridiculous in other people's conversation or behaviour; but perhaps Lady Middleton only means that the Dashwood sisters are too intelligent to be good company for her

a stupid old woman: Mrs Jennings's self-criticism might have met agreement from Elinor and Marianne in former days; but close acquaintance has made them aware of her straightforwardness, warmth, simplicity and loyalty, and (especially in contrast with such persons as Lady Middleton and Fanny Dashwood) she has gradually won their affection and respect

a misfortune:	irony at Fanny Dashwood's expense
a public school:	a large boarding school, drawing pupils from the well-to-do classes of English society. Since Jane Austen's father gave private tuition as Mr Pratt does in *Sense and Sensibility*, she is not likely to have been as biased in favour of a public-school education as Robert Ferrars shows himself to be. His behaviour and conversation are certainly no credit to Westminster School
enfranchisement:	freedom
removed:	changed their place of residence
emigrant:	person who has left his own country for another; Fanny Dashwood apparently patronises a charity that assists emigrants by finding a market for their produce and handiwork

(Volume II ends with Chapter 36 in the third and subsequent editions)

Volume III Chapter 1

Mrs Jennings informs Elinor that Anne Steele has told Fanny Dashwood of Lucy's engagement to Edward, as a result of which the Steeles have been turned out of the Dashwoods' house. Since this affair is likely to be publicly discussed, Elinor wisely informs Marianne of it in private, explaining her own attitude to Edward's actions and behaviour. For the first time Marianne realises how long and deeply Elinor has suffered a sorrow comparable to her own, and with what generosity she has turned from the indulgence of her own distress to help her sister to weather her troubles. John Dashwood informs them that Edward, confronted by his furious mother's threats of disinheritance and future persecution, and despite maternal bribes to marry the heiress Miss Morton, has honoured his promise to Lucy and has left Mrs Ferrars's house. Mrs Ferrars is reported to be making legal arrangements to settle the property that was to have been Edward's upon his younger brother, Robert.

NOTES AND GLOSSARY:

red-gum:	a childish ailment, a rash or skin eruption
no conjurer:	not a person who is able to keep a secret or an oath
I have no notion:	I don't agree with
undeceiving:	removing any mistaken ideas
office:	duty, task
apprehended:	feared
Lucy does not want sense:	Lucy is sensible

Your exclamation is very natural: John Dashwood is unaware that Marianne has been surprised, not by Edward's 'obstinacy' but by his mother's unnatural callousness

It has been dignified and liberal: not one of his listeners would agree with John Dashwood that Mrs Ferrars has behaved with calmness or generosity, but his insensitivity prevents his realising this

critique: critical discussion

Volume III Chapter 2

Elinor meets Anne Steele while walking in Kensington Gardens, and is told by her that Edward has offered to release Lucy from their engagement (since he is now to be so poor), but that she has not agreed to this; they therefore plan to marry as soon as he has taken orders and obtained a living. Lucy's letter to Elinor, however, states that Edward would not accept her offer to end their engagement.

NOTES AND GLOSSARY:

Elinor gloried in his integrity: Elinor was proud of Edward's honourable behaviour

never made any bones of: never hesitated to

huswife: a needle book or case

this bout: this time

very prettily turned: well expressed; Elinor would not have agreed with Mrs Jennings's praise of Lucy's style of letter-writing

Volume III Chapter 3

Marianne and Elinor accept the Palmers' invitation to accompany them to their home at Cleveland in Somersetshire, and go on from there to Barton. Colonel Brandon's sympathy and respect for Edward lead him to offer Edward the Delaford living. Mrs Jennings, hearing only snatches of a conversation in which the Colonel asks Elinor to convey his offer to Edward, imagines that the Colonel has asked Elinor to marry him and that she has accepted him.

NOTES AND GLOSSARY:

ennui: boredom

sang-froid: calmness

impolitic: ill-advised

Volume III Chapter 4

This is a chapter of misunderstandings. Mrs Jennings thinks the Colonel and Elinor wish Edward Ferrars, once he has been ordained, to officiate at their wedding. On being told by Elinor of Colonel Brandon's offer, Edward believes that she is about to marry the Colonel and has persuaded him to make this kind suggestion. Mrs Jennings, on being told the true state of affairs, states it as her opinion that the Delaford living (despite Colonel Brandon's doubts) is quite adequate for the support of a young couple.

NOTES AND GLOSSARY:
sagaciously: wisely, knowingly
ordination: admittance to the duties of a clergyman of the Church of England
this pleasing anticipation: this happy expectation; ironic, for the thought makes Elinor very unhappy indeed
giving ten guineas: fee paid to a clergyman who conducts a marriage service
ebullition: outburst
ninny: simpleton

Volume III Chapter 5

Elinor calls on Fanny Dashwood, and hears from John Dashwood that Mrs Ferrars has said a marriage between Edward and Elinor would have been far less of a misfortune for the family than the one now imminent, between Edward and Lucy. Robert Ferrars indulges his misplaced wit at Edward's expense, expresses contempt for Lucy, and declares that by marrying her Edward will cut himself off from all decent society— including his own. John Dashwood finds it difficult to believe that kindness is Colonel Brandon's only motive for presenting the Delaford living to Edward—who is not even a relative.

NOTES AND GLOSSARY:
Mrs Dashwood was denied: Mrs Dashwood was declared unable to see visitors
fanciful imagery: imaginary picture

Volume III Chapter 6

Elinor and Marianne travel with Mrs Jennings and Mrs Palmer to Cleveland. Marianne finds the gardens (laid out in such a way as to please romantic tastes for the picturesque) attractive, and by incautiously walking there and getting wet, catches a severe cold.

NOTES AND GLOSSARY:

offices: the kitchens and servants' quarters

its Grecian temple: a modern structure, built in imitation of an antique Greek temple. The gardens of stately homes were frequently decorated with such buildings, or with statuary and urns, carved epitaphs and pillars that claimed (or pretended to claim) an antique origin. This was part of the romantic/aesthetic taste that encouraged the cult of 'sensibility' itself, and the fashionable interest in picturesque beauty

invaluable misery: ironic allusion to the fact that Marianne's unhappiness is so precious to her that she is reluctant to lose it

blights: plant diseases

nice in his eating: fastidious, fussy about his food

epicurism: the pursuit of sensual pleasure, especially of gluttony, after Epicurus (341–270BC), a Greek philosopher who taught in Atnes from 306BC

the nicest observer of the two: the more exact observer, maker of the more careful and well-judged distinctions

Volume III Chapter 7

Marianne becomes dangerously ill, and Colonel Brandon leaves for Barton to fetch Mrs Henry Dashwood. Elinor nurses Marianne through the worst of a nearly fatal attack of pneumonia, and has just had the relief of knowing Marianne will survive her illness and that her mother will soon arrive with Colonel Brandon—when Willoughby unexpectedly arrives.

NOTES AND GLOSSARY:

apothecary: doctor, medical practitioner

a putrid tendency: infectious

emergence: emergency

succour: assistance

seisure: seizure, sickness

obviated: done away with

vestibule: entrance hall

stupor: unconscious state

unequivocal cheerfulness: undoubting joy

Volume III Chapter 8

Willoughby has been told by Sir John Middleton that Marianne is dying, and has ridden from London in the hope of explaining himself and his past actions. He tells Elinor that he had been about to ask Marianne to marry him at Barton when Mrs Smith, hearing of his seduction of Eliza Williams, ordered him to leave Allenham. Believing he had now no other hope of recouping his fortunes but to make a wealthy marriage, he had decided to forget his obligations to Marianne and her family and leave Devonshire. His letter to Marianne, he says, was written at the dictation of Miss Grey, now his wife. His obvious concern for Marianne, his regret at his past behaviour, and the unhappy marriage he has brought upon himself by his extravagance and thoughtlessness, earns Elinor's compassion and forgiveness.

NOTES AND GLOSSARY:

vehemence:	forcefulness
diabolical:	devilish
in liquor:	intoxicated
nuncheon:	light refreshment
porter:	type of beer brewed from malt
so insensible:	so insensitive, unfeeling
embarrassed:	burdened, encumbered
expatiate:	speak at length
that dreadful business:	Elinor does not wish to allude directly to Willoughby's seduction of Eliza Williams
libertine:	a licentious, immoral person
a total breach:	a complete break
memento:	keepsake, souvenir
rub through the world:	continue living, carry on
at liberty again:	free to marry again
the very he:	Willoughby here refers to Colonel Brandon

Volume III Chapter 9

Mrs Dashwood has been told by Colonel Brandon on their way to Cleveland that he loves Marianne, and she has promised to do all she can to promote his cause with Marianne when she has recovered from her illness. She tells Elinor she thinks him far more suited in character and temperament to be Marianne's husband than Willoughby could ever have been.

NOTES AND GLOSSARY:

compliance:	obedience, agreement

alarm:	fear
a pang:	a sharp sensation (of sympathy or regret)

Volume III Chapter 10

Mrs Dashwood returns to Barton with her daughters. Marianne, having had time to think about her own experiences, her recent escape from death, and Elinor's example, now plans to live a quiet life devoted to her family and to study. She expresses her sincere gratitude to Elinor, and her regret at the selfish and insensitive behaviour that must have caused her sister so much embarrassment and distress in the past. Elinor tells Marianne of her interview with Willoughby. Marianne listens with sorrowful emotion, but does not lose control of herself.

NOTES AND GLOSSARY:
contrition: penitence
softened only his protestations of present regard: did not emphasise Willoughby's declaration to her that he still loves Marianne

Volume III Chapter 11

Elinor, Marianne and Mrs Dashwood talk of Willoughby, and Marianne agrees with Elinor's sensible projection of the unhappy life she would have been likely to lead, had she married him. A servant who has been to Exeter on business brings news of Edward's marriage to Lucy Steele. Mrs Dashwood realises that Elinor is, despite all her show of calmness and self-control, deeply distressed by the news.

NOTES AND GLOSSARY:
abridge:	restrict
necessitous:	in need
hysterics:	a convulsive fit of weeping (or of laughter)
I made free:	I took the liberty

Volume III Chapter 12

Elinor awaits further news of the marriage, but receives none. Edward arrives, unexpected and alone. He tells the Dashwoods that Lucy has married his younger brother, Robert. Elinor's feelings of joy are too much for her, and she leaves the room.

NOTES AND GLOSSARY:
his air: his manner of carrying himself

rejoice in the dryness of the season: in order to save herself and everyone else from embarrassment, Elinor discusses the pleasant, dry weather they have been enjoying

spoiling both them and their sheath: Edward is under such emotional stress that he is not aware of his own actions

perplexity: confusion, wonder

Volume III Chapter 13

Edward asks Elinor to marry him, and she accepts him. He gives her an account of his earlier engagement to Lucy. John Dashwood writes to Elinor that Mrs Ferrars and Fanny have 'suffered agonies of sensibility' brought on by Robert's marriage to Lucy. He suggests that there may be a possibility of a reconciliation between Edward and his mother. As Edward and Elinor do not have enough money to marry on, Edward decides to ask Fanny and John Dashwood to attempt such a reconciliation.

NOTES AND GLOSSARY:

particularly told: described in detail

the defect of the style: faults in the manner of (her) writing

wanton: unrestrained

glebe: a portion of land assigned to a clergyman as part of his benefice or living

tythes: payment by parishioners towards the support of the local clergy

they were neither of them quite enough in love: they were not so blindly or foolishly in love as to think that ... (see the discussion between Elinor and Marianne on an adequate income upon which to marry, Volume I, Chapter 17; and Elinor's sensible words on money and marriage in Volume III, Chapter 11)

agonies of sensibility: since the reader is familiar with real sensibility (in Marianne) and knows Fanny Dashwood and Mrs Ferrars to be capable of being moved only by mercenary considerations, he will realise that John Dashwood is misusing the term and that Jane Austen is quoting him ironically and not seriously

Volume III Chapter 14

Mrs Ferrars is reconciled with Edward, who marries Elinor and settles at Delaford. In time Marianne comes to appreciate Colonel Brandon as he deserves, and they marry. Mrs Ferrars's real favour is reserved for her favourite son Robert, who is soon, through Lucy's flattery, once again in his mother's good books. The peace and happiness in which Elinor and Marianne live with their husbands at Delaford contrasts with the jealousy and ill-will that mar relationships between John and Fanny Dashwood and Robert and Lucy Ferrars in London.

NOTES AND GLOSSARY:

a proper resistance: an appropriate, correct reluctance to agree; ironic use of the word 'proper'

a sudden turn to his constitution, and carry him off: make him sick once again, and this time kill him

given with Fanny: dowry given to John Dashwood on his marriage to Fanny Ferrars

sweep: a curved carriage-drive leading up to a house

a most encouraging instance ... time and conscience: satiric irony used in a condemnatory account of Lucy Ferrars, her values and her behaviour

old acquaintance to cut: old friends she would now haughtily pretend not to see or recognise

coolness: resentment or misunderstanding

Part 3

Commentary

Jane Austen's aims

Jane Austen approached writing fiction from the eighteenth-century point of view that literature should at once instruct and entertain the reader. Her own convictions and ideas about life combine, therefore, with her lively sense of comedy to produce novels that mix seriousness with laughter. It has been said that there is a moral strain in her work so grave that it is reminiscent of Dr Samuel Johnson, the great eighteenth-century moralist whom she greatly admired. At the same time, the vividness with which she presents comic characters, scenes and dialogues reminds the reader of Henry Fielding's satiric novels and William Congreve's dramatic comedies of manners, also classics of eighteenth-century literature. In recognising the moralistic and satiric elements in her work, however, we must not overlook the fact that she was a novelist.

The English novel had its beginnings in the eighteenth century, in the work of Defoe, Richardson, Fielding, Smollet and Sterne; the nineteenth century saw the great period of its development in the fields of psychological and social realism. Although *Sense and Sensibility* shows Jane Austen's moral concern in its theme of character development and moral education as expressed through the process by which Marianne Dashwood gradually matures, moralising is not the whole of Jane Austen's interest or intention. Nor, although she ridicules the excesses of 'sensibility' and satirises the insincerity and emptiness of some aspects of upper-class social life in her time, is satire her only aim. Because of the realism with which most of its characterisation is carried out, the naturalness with which its story seems to unfold, and — most of all — the insight it yields into the inner lives of characters recognisable and acceptable to us as 'real' people living at a particular time in a particular place, *Sense and Sensibility* is a novel.

By giving her novel its particular title and appearing to appoint Elinor and Marianne Dashwood respectively as representatives in it of the qualities of 'sense' and 'sensibility' (see Part 1 for an explanation of what these terms meant in Jane Austen's time), Jane Austen has provided herself with a pattern or structure on which to build her story. Yet Elinor and Marianne are representative *characters*, and not caricatures; that is to say, Elinor does not have a monopoly of 'sense', nor is Marianne the only one to feel deeply. Despite her preoccupation with romance.

Marianne says certain things that strike the reader as extremely sensible; Volume I, Chapter 12, for instance, has Marianne state of human relationships that 'seven years would be insufficient to make some people acquainted with each other, and seven days are more than enough for others'. Can we not prove this from our own experience? Marianne proves to be wrong on the particular instance of Willoughby's character, and the plot vindicates Elinor's cautious warning that time should mature intimacy, yet some characters in the novel (Anne Steele, Lady Middleton, Sir John, Robert Ferrars, Mrs Ferrars are examples) are almost immediately assessable. Again, can the reader quarrel with Marianne for finding the Middletons boring, Mrs Jennings inquisitive, and Mrs Ferrars cruel and insulting? We might, like Elinor, wish she would control her feelings better, but we have to admit that she sees these people as they are. Similarly, Elinor is deeply sensitive; in some ways she feels more than Marianne because she does not retire into a private world of her own thoughts and fancies as Marianne quite often does. At the end of the novel, Marianne has begun to cultivate her own 'sense'; and sense has begun to control and guide the operation of sensibility in her character as it has done in Elinor's from the start of the novel.

If the two girls had been rigidly representative of 'sense' and 'sensibility' the book would not have been a novel. It would have been rightly called a 'morality', or—if comedy dominated in it over seriousness—a 'satire'. Jane Austen's urge to ridicule the contemporary craze for romantic sensibility emerges in the amusing pictures she presents of Marianne apostrophising the trees at Norland, deliberately nursing her sorrow over Willoughby's departure, and pitying Elinor for having a lover so immune to aesthetic feeling as Edward says he is. But such interests are submerged in a greater; *Sense and Sensibility* is a novel in which satiric and 'moral' elements exist side by side, alternately lighting and shading Jane Austen's central object of interest and study: the heroism of the sensitive, sensible and constant Elinor Dashwood.

Reading a novel

Reading a novel for pleasure and reading it as an examination text require an equal degree of care and attention, if the most is to be made of the matchless experience of reading a great novel for the first time. The critical commentary that follows is chiefly intended for readers who approach *Sense and Sensibility* as a literary text, and while the general reader will not, probably, need to think about the novel in the special ways essential to the student who is to write or talk about it, it is likely that some study of this section will sharpen his enjoyment of *Sense and Sensibility* and lead him to think more deeply than he otherwise would about it, and about the craft of fiction in general.

No book of notes or critical commentary, however exhaustive, can be substituted for the novel itself. Jane Austen wrote her books for the reader's enjoyment and instruction, and your response to her is the first important part of your study of her work. Therefore, before you read this critical commentary, you should have read the novel. If some lazy ignoramus has daunted you by telling you that eighteenth-century novels are 'difficult' or 'long and boring', and you have never read one before, read the general summary at the beginning of Part 2 before you read the novel. This will give you an idea of one significant element of a novel that you will need to include in any critical discussion you undertake of it: the PLOT, or chain of linked events that makes up the 'story'. Read the chapter-by-chapter synopses in Part 2 *after you have read the novel through*, or, if you wish, read the synopsis of a chapter with its notes and glossary *after you have read that particular chapter*. This is worth emphasising because there is so much in Jane Austen's writing that needs to be shared between author and reader, if possible without the interposition of a third party (however helpful or appreciative!). The synopses are intended to assist revision, to clear up difficulties, if any, and to point out features of the novel that lapse of time and differences of period, location and custom might tend to blur. *They are not substitutes for reading the novel*, and any student who treats them as such is misusing them and robbing himself of the very great pleasure of reading Jane Austen at first hand.

The plot and sub-plots

Your reading of Part 2 of these Notes will have reminded you that in addition to the MAIN PLOT (the chain of events by which Elinor and Marianne mature through experience of the world and disappointment in love) there are two linked SUB-PLOTS in the novel, both of which involve Colonel Brandon. One is the story of Elizabeth Brandon's love for the Colonel, and her later disgrace and death. The other is the story of her daughter Eliza's seduction and desertion by Willoughby, to avenge which the Colonel fights a duel with him. These sub-plots serve several purposes. The first establishes a parallel between Elizabeth Brandon and Marianne Dashwood, for Colonel Brandon who has loved Elizabeth sees a temperamental similarity to her in Marianne, and fears that their fates might be equally tragic: the sad end to which 'excess of sensibility' could lead the human personality. The second helps to deepen the aura of dissipation and unreliability that surrounds Willoughby from the time of his hasty departure from Barton; and again there is a parallel established between Eliza and Marianne, for both have trusted Willoughby and both have been betrayed by him, and Colonel Brandon's protective chivalry offers itself for the support and defence of both. The two sub-plots are interwoven with the main plot in such a way that news of the second, reaching Barton at different times, causes the hasty departure from it first of Willoughby, and then of Colonel Brandon; and the Colonel's account of the first is given to Elinor in order to help Marianne get over the shock of her betrayal by Willoughby.

Unlike many novels in which a number of sub-plots hang, attached by the slenderest of threads, upon the main plot, in *Sense and Sensibility* these subsidiary stories are fully and satisfactorily interwoven with the main chain of events. What the reader might question, in fact, is the very probability of such an interweaving: is it not too much of a coincidence that Willoughby should happen to seduce the ward of the very man who will later marry his own betrayed sweetheart? The neatness with which all loose threads are tied was a novelistic convention that could tend to rob fiction of its likeness to real life, and in later fiction (see the final chapter of *Northanger Abbey*) Jane Austen light-heartedly mocks her own observance of the code. But *Sense and Sensibility*, being the first of her novels to be published, carries upon it many marks of the writer's immaturity, and this is one of them.

Themes and structure

Four main THEMES can be distinguished in this novel, subjects upon which the author has evidently thought long and deeply and which she explores through a skilful manipulation of plot and character:

(1) a detailed consideration of the question: should the human personality be governed by sense, or by sensibility, or by a combination of both?

(2) a tracing of the process by which a youthful and immature personality matures to the point at which it can accept social responsibility in marriage or public life, and take its place in adult society

(3) a satiric exposure of contemporary social attitudes to money and marriage, and

(4) a satiric attack upon the emptiness and triviality of fashionable social life.

The novel is built upon a pattern of STRUCTURE that allows these four themes to interweave with one another. In examining the plot, we have already looked at one part of the novel's structure: for the events as retailed in the plot that trace Marianne's progress from immaturity and romanticism to maturity and good sense can be seen to help the exposition of theme (2). The stages by which Edward Ferrars grows out of his dependence upon his mother and accepts the duties of a clergyman responsible for the souls of others are also parts of the plot that contribute to the novel's structure and help the exposition of theme (2).

A second aspect of the STRUCTURE that should be noticed is the novel's division into three volumes, two of them ending on climaxes in Elinor's story (Volume I ends with her discovery of Lucy's engagement to Edward, Volume II with her conviction that their marriage is a settled thing) and the third with Elinor's marriage to Edward. Such an arrangement does much to assist the working-out of themes (1) and (2), for each climax represents a demanding test of Elinor's sense and fortitude which she survives without erosion of her generosity and sense of duty. As we watch Elinor refuse the temptation to advise Lucy against her own interests ('Your own judgement must direct you'), and encourage Colonel Brandon to give Edward the living that will make it easier for him to marry Lucy, we become aware that her good sense is supporting Elinor through despair and difficulty, and also that she is growing into an increasingly mature and responsible individual.

You should also notice that Volume I divides itself between Norland and Barton, and Volume III between Cleveland and Barton, while Volume II centres on London. The movement of the action is therefore from the country to the city, where it lingers, growing ever more detailed (in Volume II events are set out in the most minute detail of time and place almost as if the author were working from a diary or an engagement book), and then moves back to the country once more. Such a movement helps the exploration of theme (4), for Elinor and Marianne leave their happy, industrious, family life at Barton to taste the pleasures of city life ('I would have every young woman of your condition in life, acquainted with the manners and amusements of London,' says Mrs Dashwood), and find them both empty and wearying before they return disillusioned to Barton and the country.

The characters

The CHARACTERS contribute to the novel's structure in being most carefully balanced, and divided into those who seem to be all feeling, impulse and sensibility (Marianne, Mrs Henry Dashwood, Willoughby and Elizabeth Brandon) and those whose every action is governed by a preponderance of sense and caution (John Dashwood, Fanny Dashwood, Mrs Ferrars and Lucy Steele). A third group consists of characters in whose natures sense coexists with sensibility, prudence with sympathy: here we find Elinor, Colonel Brandon, and Edward Ferrars. Such a scheme assists the simultaneous exposition of themes (1) and (3), since those who are sensible are often sensible about money, and those who are reckless and impulsive seem to have difficulty in managing their financial affairs, their judgement in matters great and small being swayed by a lack of balance and objectivity.

We have now looked briefly at PLOT and THEMES, and considered the ways in which the creation of a chain of significant events, the division of the novel into three volumes, the distribution of the action between town and country, and the adoption of a carefully-balanced scheme of characterisation contribute to the STRUCTURE of *Sense and Sensibility*.

Jane Austen's handling of her CHARACTERS is so skilled and interesting, however, that it requires detailed discussion. Their apparent division into well-defined groups through whose interaction in the novel the writer debates certain ideas and explores certain moral themes is reminiscent of the techniques used in morality plays, an early form of European drama that presented moral problems and lessons on the stage for the instruction of an audience. Their cast of characters symbolised certain Christian concepts: for example, actors would appear dressed in such a manner as to represent the Seven Deadly Sins—'Gluttony', 'Sloth', 'Pride', 'Lust', 'Envy', and so on. The action of the play would demonstrate to the audience how these sins (unless checked in time) would inevitably lead a human soul to damnation, and a great deal of English fiction and drama up to the present day looks back to the ideas and methods first tried out in such mediaeval 'morality plays'. The characters in *Sense and Sensibility* could almost be characters from a morality play: Mrs Ferrars, for instance, could represent 'Pride', Fanny Dashwood 'Selfishness', John Dashwood 'Insensitivity', Lady Middleton 'Superficiality', Lucy Steele 'Cunning', Robert Ferrars 'Vanity', Sir John Middleton 'Good-Fellowship', Mrs Jennings 'Vulgarity', Anne Steele 'Stupidity'. But even though some of these characters do come close to caricature (that is, one element in their nature dominating all others to an extent that ceases to be natural), most of them have as many sides to their personalities as people do in real life. John and Fanny Dashwood do bring about a reconciliation between Edward and Mrs Ferrars, although they can gain no financial profit from doing so; Lucy Steele possesses some affection for her sister Anne, if not for anyone else; and Mrs Jennings possesses a genuine warmth and humanity that make even Marianne overlook her less attractive qualities. Jane Austen's careful balancing of 'sense' and 'sensibility' characters is not noticeable as we read the novel because of the variety of ways in which she gives her creations the illusion of real life. In detailed study of the principal characters, we will find some or all of the following methods used:

(1) characters are directly described by the narrator
(2) they present themselves in their own words, whether (*a*) in speech. or (*b*) in letters
(3) they present themselves in action
(4) they present themselves in thought
(5) we learn what they think of themselves

(6) we learn what they think of others
(7) we learn what others think of them
(8) we watch them alter over a period of time
(9) we become more intimately acquainted with them, and revise our first impressions of them.

By devising a plot which sets her characters moving in close association with each other in a setting modelled on the actual society she knew well, Jane Austen creates situations in which the behaviour and personality of each react upon and contrast with the others', and in which all have opportunities to talk to and about each other as people do in real life. In this way Jane Austen explores the themes that interest her, and while telling an entertaining and absorbing story, allows certain strongly-held moral values of her own to emerge and become established.

The individual characters

Marianne Dashwood

Marianne Dashwood's character is presented first *in direct description*: 'She was sensible and clever; but eager in every thing; her sorrows, her joys, could have no moderation. She was generous, amiable, interesting: she was everything but prudent.' Her passionate, spontaneous nature bursts out in her *words* to her mother on the subject of Edward's manner in reading poetry, in her defence of her own individualism to Elinor, in her emotional appeal to Willoughby when she sees him in London; as also in the warm, affectionate and direct style of her letter to him. In such *actions* as her indiscreet visit to Allenham, her entry into an intimate relationship with Willoughby without any formal declaration of an intention to marry on either side, her thoughtless disregard for her own health at Cleveland; and in such *behaviour* as her constant rudeness to the (admittedly boring and mediocre) people who surround her, Marianne's personality is further exposed. Marianne's *thoughts and ideas* about life, though firmly held, are ill-founded: for example, her prejudice against 'second attachments', her conviction that she will never meet a man who will satisfy her requirements, her opposition to what she calls Elinor's 'doctrine' of sensible and considerate behaviour to others, and her idea of an income that would support a married couple. She *thinks herself* justified in everything she believes and does, and will brook no opposition to her romantic principles. She is bound by the *closest affection* to her mother, who resembles her and is sympathetic to her; but she considers Edward's artistic judgement defective, and the Colonel closer to the grave than to marriage. It is obvious that those who know her well (her family, Edward, and later Colonel Brandon) respect her intelligence; those who do not, think her beautiful but unpredictable and badly behaved. In the period of three years covered by the novel we see her gradually mature, shed her prejudices, develop her sense, and cultivate a tolerance and respect for the views and personalities of others that fit her to take her place in the world as Colonel Brandon's wife.

It will be seen that in the character sketch above, the methods of characterisation numbered (1) to (8) in the preceding paragraph have been checked one by one against our reading of the novel, and where they have been found to be relevant, suitable examples have been selected to illustrate them. This is a useful method to adopt in studying characters, always keeping in mind that in particular cases additional categories may have to be included. For example, as subsidiary to (1) we should apply to Marianne's character another method, the indirect exposition of character through irony or satire. Her personality begins in laughter, for Jane Austen satirises the over-emotional heroines of much contemporary fiction through Marianne's actions and behaviour, for example her soliloquies to the trees at Norland, and her deliberate indulgence of her sorrow over Willoughby's departure. The author's tone in such passages is not the direct one of straightforward narrative: we sense suppressed laughter that is directed at Marianne even as she speaks or acts. 'And you, ye well-known trees!' she cries to the woods in their summer foliage; and when Willoughby has left her, we learn that by her the 'nourishment of grief was every day applied' to her feelings. In the scheme of the novel Marianne Dashwood is at once the satirised heroine of sensibility, and an immature child whom we watch growing up. Despite her occasional silliness she possesses a true artistic taste, a fastidious approach to language and expression, and a sensitivity so acute as to be frequently painful. Her lively intelligence and impatience with all that is trivial and mediocre fit her to be one of the novel's most outspoken critics of society's mercenary attitudes and futile pre-occupation with questions of status and etiquette, thereby assisting the exposition of themes (3) and (4). Finally, although Elinor takes the central position in the novel by virtue of her balanced personality, it is Marianne who is presented, with all her faults and virtues, in the most vivid colours. Her fragile life, brought back from the very edge of disaster, disgrace and death by chance and the combined efforts of Elinor and Colonel Brandon, tends to haunt the reader's memory long after the story has ended.

John Willoughby

John Willoughby is introduced by the author as an 'uncommonly handsome' young man, with manners both 'frank' and 'graceful'. His impetuous character emerges in his speech (' "What!" he exclaimed—

"Improve this dear cottage! No. *That* I will never consent to"'), and in both his rapid wooing of Marianne and his headlong ride to Cleveland. His thinking is hasty and undisciplined (for example he cannot think of a better way to recoup his fortunes than to abandon Marianne and marry an heiress: reform and retrenchment are not even considered for a moment), he believes that his charm can get him anything (for example the forgiveness of the Dashwoods, and the hand of Miss Grey), and his criticism of Colonel Brandon, though witty, is shallow and cruel. Everyone makes allowances for him, except Elinor who fears that his hasty judgements and self-indulgence will be his own undoing. The Eliza Williams affair indicates the presence of an unpleasant callousness beneath his charm, and Jane Austen develops his character so skilfully that the Willoughby we meet at Cleveland seems to have coarsened unattractively since we saw him say his goodbyes at Barton. This is partly effected through her presentation of his behaviour to Marianne at the London party and the letter he writes to her, and partly through the information about him that filters through to Elinor by way of Colonel Brandon and Mrs Jennings. But Willoughby is no cardboard villain, created to be replaced by Colonel Brandon as the hero in shining armour. His personal charm is very real, and we know it because Elinor (who has never been his advocate) finds herself haunted by sympathy for him and regrets on his behalf. Jane Austen's final picture of him, too, is a realistic one as he settles into middle age getting what enjoyment he can out of the life he has chosen for himself.

Mrs Henry Dashwood and Elizabeth Brandon

These are minor characters, whose 'sensibility' links them with Marianne Dashwood. Elizabeth's tragic fate is escaped by Marianne. who by the end of the novel is obviously repeating her mother's happy marriage in the second generation, having found, like her, the steady and sensible husband she needs to complement her mercurial personality. We learn from the narrator that the art of governing her feelings was 'a knowledge which [Mrs Dashwood] had yet to learn'. She says herself that she 'can feel no sentiment of approbation inferior to love', and she brings a characteristic (and endearing) warmth and eagerness to everything she says and does, whether she is criticising Mrs Ferrars's ambitions for Edward, sympathising with her daughters in their joys and sorrows, or creating that atmosphere of hospitable informality at Barton that makes the cottage so attractive to Edward, Willoughby and Colonel Brandon. Her vagaries are amusing (for example her vagueness about financial affairs, her conviction that she had perceived something unpleasing about Willoughby's eyes in the Barton days) but they should not and cannot be overlooked or minimised, for she encourages

Marianne in her extreme sensibility, and (despite Elinor's urging) fails to provide the firmness and guidance she should, as a mother, have given Marianne. The skill with which her personality is evoked indicates Jane Austen's cleverness in creating convincing family likenesses, for Elinor inherits her delicacy and considerateness for others from her mother just as Marianne inherits *her* emotionalism. There is a charmingly childish quality about Mrs Dashwood (in fact Elinor has frequently to guide her as well as Marianne!): one feels that, unlike Marianne whose experiences mature her, Mrs Dashwood will never grow up.

Since we learn all that we know of the dead Elizabeth Brandon through Colonel Brandon's melancholy conviction that she had 'the same warmth of heart, the same eagerness of fancy and spirits' possessed by Marianne, she is more a shadow upon his heart and mind than a character in the novel. He is made melancholy by his fears that Marianne might share her fate as well as her quirks of character. Since the characters in the novel who suffer like Elizabeth from an excess or misuse of sensibility do not themselves end in tragedy (Willoughby stumbles into the pit of dissoluteness and shame that waits—like the gates of Hell in the morality plays—for the unwary and sinful, but manages to get himself out again and lapse into mere ordinariness; Marianne pulls herself back from the edge; and Mrs Dashwood never even suspects that it is there), her function is to remind the reader that the dark side of sensibility must be kept in view, if only so that it may be avoided.

John Dashwood

This character is described by the narrator as 'rather cold-hearted, and rather selfish', but his ability to convince himself that he need not meet his moral obligations and the mercenary stupidity of his speeches to Elinor in Volume II characterise him more tellingly than Jane Austen's most satiric description. His ideas on the subjects of friendship and marriage (subjects close to Elinor's heart) are squalid, his readiness to toady to the wealthy Mrs Ferrars and court the rich Mrs Jennings is disgusting, and his treatment of his stepmother and sisters mean and inconsiderate. He believes that his wife, his son, and himself have a right to the attention and respect of everyone about him, he brings a trader's mentality to bear on the question of his sisters' marriages, and although we meet him often and over a period of time as the novel runs its course, our first impressions of him suffer no revision or modification. Our disgust becomes, on the contrary, intensified with each meeting; and it is only the satiric irony directed at him by his creator (turning him, with all his viciousness, into a comic character) that allows perspective to be maintained. John Dashwood's actions and opinions are, unhappily, representative of some money-minded members of the society Jane Austen knew; by making him stupid as well as mercenary she (and Elinor are able to laugh at him and his kind. And the turns of plot by which Edward Ferrars forgoes a fortune to marry Elinor, and Colonel Brandon presents a living to a man whom he respects but has no other reason to gratify, create a little world over which John Dashwood and his mercenary values have no control.

Fanny Dashwood

Fanny Dashwood is, as her creator writes, 'a strong caricature' of her husband. More selfish than he, she is not stupid, except in her inability to perceive virtue, interest, talent and elegance in her sisters-in-law. Chapter 2 in Volume I provides as detailed an exposure as anyone could desire of her character as expressed in speech. Every sentence begins with a *Certainly*, a *To be sure*, an *Undoubtedly*, an *I believe you are right*, or a *That is very true*, and each such phrase ushers in a fresh modification of her husband's original intention to give his sisters a present of £3,000. Her arguments are varied, and well-timed: she reminds him of the need to provide for their son's future, suggests that her father-in-law was not in his right mind when he asked his son to assist his family, reminds him that money once given cannot be recalled, exclaims at the luxurious life she professes to imagine Mrs Dashwood and her daughters will lead as a result of his gift, warns him of the dangers attending annuities, and complains peevishly of the superiority of Mrs Dashwood's set of china. Fanny Dashwood fans, instead of soothing, her mother's anger against Edward, and directs all her influence to keeping Elinor and her family as poor as possible and humiliating them on that account as much as she can. Her treatment of Lucy and Anne Steele is, as the forthright Mrs Jennings quite rightly says, cruel and unreasonable; and judged even by merely fashionable standards, unworthy of a woman with pretensions to refinement. The fact that she finds Lady Middleton congenial is an implied criticism of both these shallow and narrow-minded women; and her disappointment in Edward's lack of ambition is a significant mark in his favour.

Mrs Ferrars

By reason of her brief appearances in the novel, Mrs Ferrars is a minor character, but her wealth and overwhelming pride cast a shadow over it that touches every character of importance. Fanny Dashwood's selfishness derives from her (as Marianne's romantic sensibility is inherited from Mrs Henry Dashwood), and together they blight Edward's hopes of independence and a quiet life, humiliate their dependents, patronise flatterers and toadies like Anne and Lucy Steele, and victimise Mrs Henry Dashwood and her daughters. Like Fanny, Mrs Ferrars is a caricature: but of Pride, where Fanny is governed by selfishness. Money and rank are the images before which they prostrate themselves, and Jane Austen is too realistic to pretend that their influence does not matter. Mrs Ferrars's threat to 'do all in her power to prevent [Edward's] advancing in ... any profession' of his choice was no idle one. Preferment depended largely upon interest and patronage and, branded by his mother's ill will, Edward is fortunate to find an advocate in Elinor and a benefactor in Colonel Brandon through whose assistance he can make his own way. Distasteful as the idea is to them, Edward and Elinor must effect a reconciliation with Mrs Ferrars before they can afford to marry; and it is Jane Austen's final ironic condemnation of Mrs Ferrars that while she never really warms towards Edward and Elinor, Robert and Lucy become her 'favourite' children.

Lucy Steele

Lucy Steele draws upon herself one of the most savagely satiric comments Jane Austen ever gave to a character of her own creation: 'The whole of Lucy's behaviour in the affair, and the prosperity which crowned it, therefore, may be held forth as a most encouraging instance of what an earnest, an unceasing attention to self-interest, however its progress may be apparently obstructed, will do in securing every advantage of fortune, with no other sacrifice than that of time and conscience.' Lucy, like John and Fanny Dashwood, enjoys wealth and the favour of Mrs Ferrars. Domestic happiness, and tranquillity of the kind enjoyed by Edward and Elinor, and Marianne and Colonel Brandon is not to be hers; but she has got what she hoped for out of life, and with the same realism that made her grant Willoughby a tolerable contentment, Jane Austen allows Lucy to be as happy as she can with it. The depths of Lucy's character are known only to Elinor. Mrs Jennings thinks her 'a good-hearted girl as ever lived', Sir John thinks her 'monstrous pretty, and so good humoured and agreeable', Marianne thinks her an ill-bred bore. Edward's growing distaste for her is complicated by his own feelings of guilt. Her face her only fortune, Lucy schemes for her own advancement; and when she suspects that Elinor stands in her way, takes cunning and unscrupulous steps to eliminate her. Her lack of education and the coarseness of her mind and moral standards are simultaneously caught by Jane Austen in speech after speech of Lucy's to Elinor; and her letters to Elinor and to Edward are minor masterpieces of deceit and hypocrisy. The only person to whom Lucy shows any affection is her elder sister, Anne. But their relationship is flawed by mutual mistrust and contempt, and compares most unfavourably with the loving respect Elinor and Marianne have for one another. Lucy, as Elinor admits, 'does not want sense'; but like John and Fanny Dashwood and Mrs Ferrars, Lucy possesses only that kind of mercenary self-interest which, in shutting out humanity and sympathetic feeling, is identical in Jane Austen's world with stupidity.

Elinor Dashwood

Elinor Dashwood is the novel's centre. The responsibility of representing 'sense', of advising her impulsive mother, and of guiding her romantic sister towards maturity sometimes seems too much for a girl who is only nineteen years old when the novel begins. But she does not escape Jane Austen's ironic eye, and such touches of humour help to make her character convincing and human. She is sensitive and observant, and is therefore an excellent medium through whom to communicate information to the reader. For Elinor is not easily duped or misled. She sees through the duplicity of Lucy Steele and the thinly-disguised politeness of Fanny Dashwood. She observes Willoughby carefully, and alone among his acquaintances at Barton fears for his future career. She understands Colonel Brandon's feelings almost as well as he does himself, and has matured enough in her knowledge of the world by the end of the novel to take accurately the measure of Willoughby's irresponsible and unreliable character. At the same time, as her creator makes clear, 'her feelings were strong'. Her sensitivity, though not so acutely agonising as Marianne's, causes John Dashwood's mean-minded remarks to her to resound in our minds with their full complement of squalidness. She reacts strongly when Lucy viciously attacks Marianne, and Robert Ferrars patronises Edward. Sense and sensibility, reason and passion, mind and heart complement each other in Elinor. Where Marianne exemplifies the weakening tendencies of excessive emotionalism, Elinor offers a positive alternative; for through her disciplined, voluntary efforts to control her emotions and regulate her behaviour, practising consideration· for others without sacrificing honour or principle, she achieves true strength and balance of character.

Edward Ferrars and Colonel Brandon

Both these characters suffer somewhat from being presented by their creator in negative terms. Edward is *not* (his future mother-in-law observes with pleasure) like his sister Fanny; Marianne finds 'something wanting', and judges him devoid of a striking appearance, lively expression and real taste. Colonel Brandon is thought to be, at thirty-five. too old for marriage (by Marianne), and is even less like a romantic hero than is Edward. Both these characters are presented in this way so that they might not detract from the impressive flourish with which the handsome and personable Willoughby takes the centre of the stage in Volume I, Chapter 9. As the novel progresses, however, the reader comes to know each of them better, respect Edward for the delicate sense of honour which makes him keep his promise to Lucy, and give the Colonel full credit for the delicacy and generosity he shows to Marianne and Edward at the time they need help most. Like Marianne, Edward has to mature. He has to throw off the restricting carapace his mother has built around him, and start life on his own. His progress to independence and maturity, therefore, contributes to Jane Austen's exposition of theme (2), while the Colonel's generosity to those in need provides a moral standard with which Jane Austen contrasts the meanness of John and Fanny Dashwood and Mrs Ferrars, thus contributing to theme (3). Both men resemble Elinor Dashwood in possessing characters that harmoniously reconcile sense and sensibility, and together with her they form a third group centred upon Delafield. There, in contrast to the empty noise of Barton Park and the selfish ill-nature to be found at Norland and at Robert Ferrars's London establishment, good sense and sympathy create an alternative world and a congenial society.

Mrs Jennings

Mrs Jennings is a minor character of great interest. Her inquisitiveness and vulgarity irritate Elinor and Marianne when they first meet her at Barton, but she develops as a personality on closer acquaintance in London. Her loyalty to her old friends, her genuine kindness to Marianne, her sympathy for Edward when she hears of his disinheritance—these are good points that begin increasingly to out-weigh the bad until by the end of the novel she has become—although still comic—an old and valued acquaintance. This is characterisation that goes beyond balance and arrangement, to imitate real life.

Sir John and Lady Middleton

These are minor characters whose passion for entertaining does much to set the characters moving in sociable patterns, and whose hospitality is so undiscriminating and lacking in intelligent interest that a good deal of satire at their expense illuminates theme (4). Sir John judges men as sportsmen rather than as human beings; his wife estimates women according to the time they are willing to sacrifice to the whims of her spoiled children. He is never happier than when playing host to a large crowd; she loves entertaining, but on a more exclusive and formal pattern. Elinor is always polite to them, Marianne (who thinks them ignorant and contemptible) is off-hand or downright rude. They are like Mrs Ferrars, in being caricatures that do not develop. But, like her, they are essential to the novel; for from their fear of being left to each other's company arise the many social opportunities provided for Willoughby and Marianne to progress rapidly in their acquaintance. When the Middletons go to London, the circles of their relations and friends widen and interlock. Jane Austen's talent for 'collecting . . . people delightfully' is demonstrated in her hint that Lady Middleton and Fanny Dashwood are certain to get on. The Steeles' fawning, flattering ways charm Fanny as they have pleased Lady Middleton, and from the meetings prompted by such flocking together and social intermingling spring a series of exchanges rich in ironic comedy.

Anne Steele

Anne Steele, like Mrs Jennings, is a character who comes to life in her vivid speech. Silly and vulgar, she provides Lucy with a constant source of embarrassment. Like Lucy she uses flattery to get on, but aims far lower, and constantly reveals in her endless flow of talk the poverty that Lucy is too cunning and too proud to admit. She is not, though supremely comic in her foolish vulgarity, in the novel solely on that account. Her silliness is essential to the plot, for it leads her to reveal Lucy's secret to Fanny Dashwood and so bring about the crisis by which Edward is disinherited. Throughout the novel, her relationship with Lucy is implicitly compared with that of the Dashwood sisters; and the eagerness with which she pursues 'smart beaux' contrasts with the restraint and delicacy Elinor brings to her relationship with Edward.

Robert Ferrars

Robert Ferrars is a caricature. He has pretensions to 'good taste', and would like to be considered a connoisseur of art and architecture, but his contemptuous dismissal of his much worthier brother Edward shows that he does not know how to value character. He encourages his mother in her unreasonable rage at Edward's refusal to abandon his promise to Lucy, and is perfectly ready to cut Edward out of his own life for ever. Marrying him is the (dreadful) price Lucy must pay for the wealth and consequence she craves.

Mr and Mrs Palmer

Mr and Mrs Palmer, too, are caricatures. They are amusing in a limited way, and serve a function in the novel only by swelling the crowd of acquaintances Elinor and Marianne must mix with in London, and by providing a house (Cleveland) midway between London and Barton where Marianne can fall ill and Willoughby can interview Elinor. The presence in a novel of such characters as these is a sign of Jane Austen's comparative immaturity at the time she published it. Mr and Mrs Palmer have not, unlike Anne Steele, been satisfactorily woven into the fabric of the novel.

The setting

Jane Austen sets her characters moving in a SETTING that is modelled closely upon the real life of the society she knew. She deliberately excludes from her work all material that is merely sensational or decorative, however intrinsically interesting or historically important, concentrating her attention upon the thoughts and feelings, motives and prejudices of men and women. The numerous social engagements that bore Marianne at Barton and in London (once Willoughby is no longer with her to engage all her attention!) faithfully reflect the typical events that characterised an autumn in the country and a winter season in London. By moving her principal characters from Barton to London and back again, she simultaneously explores theme (4) and provides the reader with variety of setting and interest. But she never dwells on details of a landscape or an interior for their own sake: her description of Barton Cottage (and Robert Ferrars's later stupidities on the subject of magnificent country cottages) serve to remind us that the right-thinking Mrs Dashwood and her children prefer the inconveniences of a cottage to the luxuries of Norland (now soured for them by the presence there of Fanny Dashwood); and the artistically landscaped garden at Cleveland is an appropriate setting for Marianne's final, and very nearly tragic, indulgence of her romantic sensibility. The smallest details of life as she knew it are pressed into service in revealing character or helping the progress of the plot: Lady Middleton's endless games of casino and whist provide the smooth social surface under cover of which Lucy Steele delivers, one by one, the deadly blows she hopes will cripple Elinor, and Willoughby, by his behaviour to her at the party, wounds Marianne to the heart. Elinor's punctiliousness in performing the tedious social duty of calling on Fanny Dashwood mirrors, in a small way, the unselfishness and sense of duty she brings to the major problems in her life.

Some critics have seen Jane Austen's refusal to let her characters venture beyond the everyday round of English middle-class life as a limitation upon her art. But all the evidence shows that it was a self-imposed limitation: she had knowledge and experience of such exciting contemporary events as the Napoleonic wars and the Reign of Terror in

France (through her brothers, who fought in the first, and a cousin whose husband died in the second), yet she did not choose to draw upon them in any substantial way. Invited, with an assurance of royal patronage, to write a historical novel, she politely refused. She compared her own work to miniature painting on ivory 'on which I work with so fine a Brush, as produces little effect after much labour'. Regulating the outward activities of her characters by social customs that were well known to her readers, Jane Austen allows us to see through such externals to the endless variety in human nature and the endlessly interesting differences in human behaviour. It is clear from our reading of *Sense and Sensibility* that such so-called 'limitations' of setting do not hinder the raising of fundamental moral issues, for example the nature of moral responsibility, the education of the human personality, the justice and morality of established social attitudes and customs. They permit heroes and heroines to emerge in fiction who are more, not less, heroic because honesty is their only armour and wit the only weapon with which they can defend themselves. Jane Austen's comment in a letter written to a novel-writing niece comes directly from her own experience as a novelist: 'Three or four Families in a Country Village is the very thing to work upon.'

Ironic satire

Jane Austen's moral values are seldom directly stated. They usually emerge indirectly, through her approval of and sympathy for characters who abide by them, or through the operation of her characteristic brand of IRONIC SATIRE. Irony is defined as 'a figure of speech in which the intended meaning is the opposite of that expressed by the words used'. In the chapter-by-chapter synopses in Part 2 you will have found some of the passages in which Jane Austen makes particularly notable use of irony marked for your attention. With this writer, however, irony is not so much a figure of speech she resorts to from time to time, as a habitual point of view and style of writing. Jane Austen was thirty-six years old when she published *Sense and Sensibility*, and her private letters reveal that there was much she disliked and resented about the conditions of her life. The smallness of society in a Hampshire village (and its small-mindedness too, perhaps) provided few outlets for a critical intelligence such as hers, and some of her private opinions appear, suitably veiled in irony, in her novels. When we read *Sense and Sensibility*, there are certain sections in which we, sharing Elinor's point of view, feel particularly oppressed, helpless and irritated. See Volume II, Chapter 11, for instance, where Elinor is forced by the rules of social etiquette and her own sense of duty to listen politely to John Dashwood's persistent application of material values to the human relationships of friendship and marriage. His opinions are so disgusting that they almost cease to be comic. What keeps them so is Elinor's steadfast refusal to retort, her determination in warding off and (as far as she can) ignoring his point of view, and her ability to find his stupidity amusing. Hers is, in fact, an *ironic* point of view. Examine her response to him:

> 'You may guess, after all these expenses, how very far we must be from being rich, and how acceptable Mrs Ferrars's kindness is.'
> 'Certainly,' said Elinor; 'and assisted by her liberality, I hope you may yet live to be in easy circumstances.'

She knows, and we know, that John Dashwood and his wife have grown rich at her expense. He knows it, too. Her words are polite, but a less insensitive person than her brother might have suspected that they carry a sting. As it is (John being so stupid) Elinor is safe—he gravely agrees with her! This is the game habitually played by Elinor, not for amusement as Lady Middleton plays cards, but for survival. Irony is the only weapon with which she can defend her self-respect when either her family's reputation or her personal code of values is attacked by such persons as John Dashwood or Lucy Steele.

Since the novel is chiefly presented through Elinor's thoughts and observations, the narrative itself takes on this characteristically ironic flavour: superficially grave or conformist, but contemptuous and even condemnatory when one looks deeper. Here are some examples:

> On every formal visit a child ought to be of the party, by way of provision for discourse. (Volume I, Chapter 6)

> Sir John was a sportsman, Lady Middleton a mother. He hunted and shot, and she humoured her children; and these were their only resources. (Volume I, Chapter 7)

> A lucky contraction of the brow had rescued her countenance from the disgrace of insipidity, by giving it the strong characters of pride and ill nature. (Volume II, Chapter 12)

> Elinor had some difficulty here to refrain from observing, that she thought Fanny might have borne with composure, an acquisition of wealth to her brother, by which neither she nor her child could be possibly impoverished. (Volume III, Chapter 5)

Reading these passages, the reader can see that though they are all ironic (that is, represent a characteristic double-view of seriousness and laughter, politeness and resentment), some are more forceful than others. The last (and the description of Lucy Steele quoted in the character study of her given in this Part) are particularly strong: anger and resentment are very thinly masked by Jane Austen's calm, composed narrative tone. So we might distinguish between a simple, or easy irony (where not very much is at stake, and the author is amused but not very deeply concerned) and savage or satiric irony (where certain valued convictions or principles are placed in jeopardy). When her fidelity to truth requires her to paint the worldly success enjoyed by such worthless people as Fanny Dashwood and Lucy Steele at the expense of the sensitive or high-principled, Jane Austen resorts to irony in much the same way as Elinor Dashwood resorts to a 'look':

> Elinor, while she waited in silence, and immovable gravity, the conclusion of such folly, could not restrain her eyes from being fixed on [Robert Ferrars] with a look that spoke all the contempt it excited. It was a look, however, very well bestowed, for it relieved her own feelings, and gave no intelligence to him. (Volume III, Chapter 5)

'It relieved her own feelings, and gave no intelligence to him.' The ironic mode of writing affords the writer a vent for intense feeling which, if openly or explicitly expressed, would alter the character of her work, turning it from fiction into a sermon or a pamphlet. Many of Jane Austen's readers over the years have (like Robert Ferrars in this scene) failed to recognise the contempt hidden beneath her polite tone. Having read her superficially or hastily, they miss the full range of her purpose and her subtlety as a writer, and think her a harmlessly amusing purveyor of social comedy. By such she has been called 'quaint', 'charming', 'whimsical' and 'delightful'; but although her lively sense of the comic calls forth the amusement of every reader, a careful one will not miss the irony implicit in nearly every sentence of *Sense and Sensibility*, or fail to respond to the urgent protest Jane Austen lodges through it at the immorality and injustice of certain accepted social values. Satire has been defined as a composition in which the vices or follies of the time are held up to ridicule. While many writers might criticise people or customs, a true satirist is one who makes vice and folly ridiculous and laughable with the intention of encouraging society to rid itself of such faults. Jane Austen is a novelist whose fiction contains elements of satire, and whose characteristic technique includes an ironic style of writing that arises from a habitually ironic point of view.

The language

Jane Austen would never have been referred to as a satirist or praised for her skilful use of irony if she had been careless or uncritical in her use of language. In reading *Sense and Sensibility* you may have noticed how often the characters discuss STYLE, that is, their own or others' use of language. In Volume I, Chapter 9, Marianne objects to Sir John Middleton's expressions for three reasons: *(i)* they are 'gross', that is, stupid and unrefined *(ii)* 'illiberal', that is, ungenerous to human nature in general, and to women in particular *(iii)* time has made them stale and trite. Despite Marianne's other faults and weaknesses, her fastidiousness regarding the use of language is shared by the author, as it is by Elinor, Edward, Colonel Brandon and (under Marianne's influence) even Willoughby. They use language carefully and memorably themselves, and are openly or inwardly critical of its ill-use by others. Colonel Brandon's polite, yet sympathetic reply to Mrs Jennings's vulgar question in Volume II, Chapter 4, regarding her daughter Charlotte's 'fine size' indicates his maturity. He will not, unlike Marianne in her reproof of Sir John, show his disgust, but instead replies in such a way as to demonstrate *(a)* his refusal to descend to Mrs Jennings's level by answering her in her own style, and *(b)* his readiness to overlook her crudeness on account of his appreciation of the true goodness of her character. Edward Ferrars's restraint in his use of aesthetic terminology in Volume I, Chapter 18, directs our attention to some of the weaknesses in contemporary 'jargon' relating to appreciation of the picturesque; his comment, therefore, on the 'defect' of Lucy's letter-writing style in Volume III, Chapter 13, is very much in character. The skill with which Jane Austen differentiates characters through their respective styles of speaking and writing is a sign that her choice of language and her use of it are most carefully carried out. The degree to which an Austen character can select and use words effectively is a reliable clue to the quality of his judgement in other and larger matters. In the owner of an uneducated or pretentious style we may look (although we may not always find them, for example Mrs Jennings, or Robert Martin in *Emma*) for moral flaws of varying seriousness. Willoughby despises his own letter to Marianne, asking Elinor what she thinks 'of my wife's style of letter-writing? delicate—tender—truly feminine—was it not?' (Volume III, Chapter 8). Mrs Jennings, who has not enough education herself to perceive the flaws in Lucy's letter to Elinor, considers her on the evidence of that letter to be 'a good-hearted girl as ever lived', and believes the 'pretty' letter to do 'Lucy's head and heart great credit' (Volume III, Chapter 2). Jane Austen's attention to STYLE and diction, whether in writing narrative, letters or dramatic dialogue, is an important part of her technique as a novelist, continually rendering more effective the realism of PLOT and incident, the exploration through character and action of major THEMES, the liveliness and verisimilitude of CHARACTER, the achievement of a balanced but unobtrusive STRUCTURE, the evocation of a convincing and functional SETTING, and the ceaseless play, over all, of all characteristically satiric IRONY.

Part 4

Hints for study

(i) Organising your study

It is suggested that if you are preparing for an examination you might use these Notes as follows: (*i*) Read Part 1 carefully, and make certain you understand the explanations given in it of the terms 'sense', 'sensibility', and 'taste'. (*ii*) Read the novel with the aid of the general summary, the synopses, and the notes supplied in Part 2. As you reach the end of each volume, use the revision questions in section (iv) of this Part to refresh your memory of what you have been reading, and accustom yourself to thinking about the novel in a critical and analytical way. (*iii*) Read Part 3. This is designed to give you various headings or categories, which facilitate discussion of different aspects of the novel; each aspect is illustrated from the novel. Prepare a summary of Part 3, supplying where necessary, or possible, your own illustrations. The summary you prepare might look like this:

(a) Plot

---

(1) Main plot:
  (*a*) Marianne's progress from romantic immaturity to maturity
  (*b*) Elinor's progress from inexperience to a better knowledge of the world
  (*c*) Edward's progress from dependence and immaturity to independence and maturity
(2) Sub-plots:
  (*a*) Elizabeth Brandon's disgrace and death
  (*b*) Eliza William's seduction by Willoughby

(b) Themes

---

(1) Sense, sensibility, or a combination of both to govern the human personality?
(2) Moral education
(3) Satiric examination of eighteenth-century attitudes to money and marriage
(4) Satiric exposure of fashionable social life

(c) Structure

(1) Division of novel into three volumes assists the working-out of themes (1) and (2) above.
(2) Variation of setting and movement of characters between Barton–London–Barton assists working-out of theme (4).
(3) Division of characters into three main groups
   (*a*) predominance of 'sense'
   (*b*) predominance of 'sensibility'
   (*c*) 'sense'/'sensibility' in harmony
   helps working out of themes (1) and (3).

(d) Characters

(1) 'Morality play' element in Jane Austen's characterisation
(2) Satiric element in Jane Austen's characterisation
(3) Elements of psychological insight and verisimilitude in Jane Austen's characterisation
(4) Methods of characterisation:
   (*a*) narrator's description: (*i*) straightforward, (*ii*) ironic
   (*b*) through style of expression: (*i*) in conversation, and (*ii*) in letters
   (*c*) through action and behaviour
   (*d*) through characters' ideas on general subjects
   (*e*) through their opinions of others
   (*f*) through their opinions of themselves
   (*g*) through other's opinions of them
   (*h*) through changes observed in them over a period of time
   (*i*) through closer acquaintance that calls for a revision of first impressions
(5) The 'predominance of sense' group:
   (*a*) Lucy Steele (*major character*)
   (*b*) John Dashwood (*minor*)
   (*c*) Fanny Dashwood (*minor*)
   (*d*) Mrs Ferrars (*minor, caricature*)
(6) The 'predominance of sensibility' group:
   (*a*) Marianne Dashwood (*major*)
   (*b*) John Willoughby (*major*)
   (*c*) Mrs Henry Dashwood (*minor*)
   (*d*) Elizabeth Brandon (*minor*)
(7) The 'sense and sensibility' group:
   (*a*) Elinor Dashwood (*major, and central character*)
   (*b*) Edward Ferrars (*major*)
   (*c*) Colonel Brandon (*major*)

(8) Minor characters:
   (*a*) Mrs Jennings—*dramatically developed, and with psychological insight*
   (*b*) Anne Steele—*dramatically developed, and with psychological insight*
   (*c*) Sir John and Lady Middleton—*caricatures that illuminate theme* (4)
   (*d*) Robert Ferrars—*caricature that illuminates themes* (3) *and* (4)
   (*e*) Mr and Mrs Palmer—*caricatures*

(e) Setting

(1) Re-creation of eighteenth-century social life in faithful and accurate detail
(2) Careful observation and re-creation in detail of scenes and objects
(3) Deliberate limitation of scene and setting to achieve particular artistic aims

(f) Style

(1) Effectiveness of Jane Austen's precise diction in every aspect of her work, and especially in characterisation and narration
(2) Irony used as a means of expressing moral convictions
(3) Irony used as a means of satirically exposing flaws in contemporary society
(4) Differentiation of character through distinctive styles of speaking
   · or writing

Here is a basic scheme that you can adapt for your own use. The divisions (a) to (f) given above include all the chief points upon which you could base a discussion of any aspect of *Sense and Sensibility*. To these you might add some or all of the following:

(g) Jane Austen's life

(h) Jane Austen's method of writing (include comments made by the novelist on her own style and techniques)

(i) Textual history of *Sense and Sensibility*

(j) The structure of eighteenth-century society, with special reference to
   (1) social ranks and divisions
   (2) money and land
   (3) the position of women

(k) Critical opinions of Jane Austen's fiction

The divisions (g) to (k) above constitute 'background' information. The material they contain is unlikely to form the substance of an examination answer on the novel, but the range and interest of an answer on Jane Austen's style would certainly be widened if, for instance, you could introduce a sentence or two from comments made by the author herself on the effects she aimed at in writing fiction. The information required for divisions (g) and (i) will be found in Part 1 of these Notes, and some of the material you will need for divisions (h) and (k) will be found introduced in Parts 1, 2 and 3. Look up a reference work on the literary and social history of England for the material you will need for the rest; it will also give you all you need for division (j) that the novel itself does not provide.

(ii) Selecting quotations

A well-chosen quotation, aptly introduced to illustrate a point made in your discussion, does a great deal to demonstrate your familiarity with the text. In answering questions on literature texts, quotations could be usefully introduced:

(a) *to illustrate* a statement made by you
(b) *to support* a statement made by you (this is likely to be a critic's viewpoint that you find agrees with yours)
(c) *to initiate a discussion* (this is likely to be a critical viewpoint with which you do not agree, but which you wish to discuss in the course of your answer because it sheds light on the topic under consideration)
(d) *to provide* yourself with an opportunity to show your understanding of a writer's themes and techniques through *critical analysis of a quoted passage.*

It is obvious that (b) and (c) will be selected by you in the course of your reading of criticism on the novel. For (a), read the novel a second time with the scheme you have prepared beside you, and *for each point in it select one, or preferably two or three, illustrative quotations.* These should be brief, for they must be accurately memorised. Write them into your scheme at the relevant points. For (d), consider division (f) (style) in your scheme. It is in discussions of an author's style and technique that practical analysis and criticism are most useful and effective. Ask yourself which aspects of Jane Austen's literary technique interest you. Her satire of Marianne's romanticism? Her exposition of character through dialogue? Her exposition of character through epistolary (letter-writing) style? Her satire of fashionable social life? Her dramatisation of incident? Her employment of irony for satiric purposes? Now select a passage appropriate to the technique of your choice that is (a) representative of her very best efforts in that particular technique, (b) short enough to be memorised, (c) long enough and rich enough in good material to give you scope for a discussion that covers all essential points.

Let us suppose the aspects of Jane Austen's literary technique listed above interest you equally, and that you would like an opportunity to write about them in the course of an answer, if the opportunity arises. Here are some suggestions regarding passages for quotation and critical analysis:

(1) *Satire of romanticism:* Volume I, Chapter 5, 'And you, ye well-known trees! . . . enjoy you?'

(2) *Character exposed through dialogue:* Volume I, Chapter 2, 'They will live so cheap! . . . to give *you* something.'

(3) *Character exposed through a letter:* Volume III, Chapter 2, 'I am sure you will be glad to hear . . . to assist us.'

(4) *Satire of fashionable life:* Volume I, Chapter 7, 'Sir John was a sportsman . . . good-breeding of his wife.'

(5) *Dramatisation of incident:* Volume III, Chapter 2, 'Very well indeed! . . . head and heart great credit.' Also Volume III, Chapter 1, 'She fell into violent hysterics . . . I pity *her*.'

(6) *Satiric irony:* Volume III, Chapter 14, 'The whole of Lucy's behaviour . . . time and conscience.'

When you analyse these or any other passages critically, comment first on the DICTION, that is, on words or phrases that are especially striking, and which reinforce the point you are making; then on the RHYTHM of the passage (particularly important if it is satiric, or represents speech); then on the ideas or IMAGES introduced. See section (iv) of this Part for some examples that you may find useful. Part of your preparation for the examination should be *the writing of critical analyses of the longer passages* you have selected. Make these brief but pithy, and into them put your own views of Jane Austen's literary style and methods, making sure they are well supported by the passage you are discussing. Should the examination question give you an opportunity to use one or more of these in your answer, you will be able to draw on your memory of them without much effort, thus saving yourself the anxiety of 'wondering what to say' when the minutes are ticking away, and giving yourself the advantage of presenting in an answer, well thought-out, properly formulated, yet *original* ideas. Each such passage you present, if well executed and appropriate, helps to make your answer stand out from among the rest, for it demonstrates the fact that your reading of the text has been thoughtful, critical, appreciative and intelligent.

(iii) Arranging your material

Questions on literature texts are usually of five types:

(1) Those that test your knowledge of the plot and the order of events in it, for example, 'On what occasions and in what ways did Mr John Dashwood make himself offensive to his sister Elinor?', or 'What are the incidents in the novel which help to mature Marianne Dashwood?'

(2) Questions on background, for example, 'What have you learned from this book about the lives women led in the late eighteenth century?'

(3) General questions that call for an over-all survey of the work, for example, 'Estimate Jane Austen's achievement as a novelist.'

(4) Questions that focus on a particular aspect of a writer's achievement, for example, 'Give your estimate of the character of (a) Marianne Dashwood, (b) Lucy Steele'; 'Illustrate Jane Austen's skill in dialogue by giving an account of any two conversations in the novel'; 'What part is played by irony in the novel?'

(5) Context questions, for example, 'Relate the following passage to its context, and comment on any points of interest: "He would have had a wife of whose temper he could make no complaint, but he would have been necessitous— always poor; and probably would soon have learnt to rank the innumerable comforts of a clear estate and good income as of far more importance, even to domestic happiness, than the mere temper of a wife."'

Before discussing techniques for answering questions of each of the above types, here are some suggestions on general procedure to keep in mind:

Do give yourself ten minutes or so to read the examination paper through carefully, and prepare a plan of action before beginning to write.

Do make sure *how many questions* you are required to answer, and mark off on your paper before beginning to write *which questions you will answer*, and *the order in which you hope to answer them.* Since you will find yourself gaining confidence after the first few minutes of writing a good answer, deal with what you think will be your best answer first.

Do jot down on rough paper (which should be provided—if not, ask for it, or rule off a section at the back of your answer-book and mark it 'Answer Plan') before beginning to write your answer, *a list of points you intend to use, in the order that you expect to use them.* Do this for each answer.

Do keep your handwriting neat, and deal with each point in an orderly manner before proceeding (with a new paragraph) to the next. Proper, accurate paragraphing allows your examiner to see at a glance that you not only have brought a great deal of thought to your answer, but have arranged your ideas in a methodical manner.

Don't relate the plot of the novel, unless the question specifically requires it. To do so in a general question is a complete waste of time which you could devote to getting several valuable points stated.

Don't forget to use quotation marks when introducing the opinion of another writer; and state your reference. To pass another writer's work off as your own, whether deliberately or by accident, is unforgivable and will be penalised by the examiner.

Don't leave answers incomplete, or your paper unfinished. Draw a line at the end of each completed answer as you finish it, and another at the very end of your completed paper. If you find that you are running out of time and will not be able to treat the question as fully as you wish, say so, and insert at this juncture a list of the points you would have used, in the order in which you would have used them. Do not scribble a helpless 'no time', or stop in mid-sentence. Having written in your list of points, draw a line across the page, to indicate that you have completed your paper.

Don't trust to luck regarding either time or inspiration. Make sure the clock in the hall is working, and that it tells the right time, or depend on your own accurate wrist-watch. Time your answers, remembering to make allowance for the fact that in a paper requiring four answers, your first two answers are likely to take up more of your time than the last two. Try to divide your time as equally as possible among the answers: the result will be a more balanced paper. As regards inspiration, some people find they work very well under examination pressure. These are invariably people who have prepared themselves carefully beforehand. Make sure you are among them.

In order to answer any examination question fully and effectively, prepare yourself by arranging the knowledge you have gathered from your reading of the novel, and from this and any other book, in the form of a summary. Use the scheme provided in section (i) of this Part, and adapt it to your needs. Insert at the appropriate points brief reminders of the illustrative quotations you have chosen, the critical opinions you wish to refer to, and the passages on which you have carried out original critical analysis. You might use different-coloured inks for the headings and sub-headings, if this helps you to secure a better visual memory of your summary. The final result should be *brief* (four sides of quarto or foolscap paper would be quite sufficient), *clearly set out* (a typed or printed summary is easier to take in at a glance than flowing handwriting), and *represent to you, in capsule form, material which you have already grasped, and thoroughly assimilated.*

Some students treat summaries as answers, which is most unwise. Those who do, tend to begin their written answers to any and every question with the first sentence in their summary. The question might call for a discussion of satiric irony in the novel; but the student, stolidly working through his prepared summary, will (if he is using the scheme prepared in section (i) in an unimaginative and unintelligent manner) begin his answer with the sentence 'The main plot of the novel centres on the progress of certain characters to maturity from a state of youthful immaturity or dependence. . . .' or even 'Jane Austen was born in Steventon in 1775'! He will, of course, gain no marks, *since he obviously has made no attempt to deal with the question.*

Your summary is *not* a condensed or potted answer. *It is, on the other hand, a compendium of all the material you will need for any answer* (see section (iv) of this Part for lists of specimen questions and suggestions for the best ways of answering them), arranged in such a way that you can draw from it what you want when you want it.

This is how to use your summary. With your summary in mind, read the paper carefully, and select the questions you intend to answer. Unless they are general questions (in which case you might need to draw on all the points in your summary), you will find that the particular problems posed relate to single sections of your summary, for example to PLOT, THEMES, SETTING, CHARACTER, STRUCTURE, STYLE, or BACKGROUND. Mentally place this section at the head of your list of the points you will use in your answer. Now visualise the rest of your summary, asking yourself which of the remaining points (or which parts of them) have some connection with the problem. Consider your 'practical criticism' passages: which of them could you introduce appropriately and usefully? Jot down in your 'Answer Plan' a list of the points you will use, in the right order. Mentally review your summary once more, to make sure you have omitted nothing of value. Now write your answer.

Remember that the work of a great writer is usually so unified that each part of it is connected with its other parts. In discussing Jane Austen's fiction, for example, consideration of her characters will inevitably lead to a discussion of the themes those characters represent, and of the stylistic techniques she employs to make them realistic and convincing. An examination question that appears to focus on a single aspect of her work may well be best answered by *dealing with that aspect first and at length,* and then by including discussion of related aspects of her work, but giving these aspects the lesser significance that the question demands. A sense of proportion in these matters is well worth developing.

If you have prepared yourself well, used your summary sensibly, and deployed the points and illustrations you have gathered to the best advantage, the result will be a well organised, accurate and comprehensive answer in which the various points made are logically connected, aptly illustrated, suitably supported by a quotation or two from contemporary criticism of standing, and illuminated by some fresh and original critical analysis of specific passages.

(iv) Specimen questions

Context questions

From an examiner's point of view a context question tests a candidate's understanding of the text; from a student's point of view, answering such questions is an admirable practical exercise in critical analysis and the use of technical terms. You will find below, two specimen questions of this type, and two 'model' answers. You will see at once that in answering these questions, the same technique has been used as that suggested in section (iii), that is, working from a prepared summary Capital letters have been used for some words, to remind the reader that they signal points that have been drawn from the summary.

In answering a context question, it is necessary first to identify the source of the passage, that is, to state specifically from which part of the novel it has been taken. This does not, of course, mean that a volume-and-chapter reference must be given, but one should be able to state what events immediately preceded it, and what will immediately follow it, identifying at the same time any speaker whose words are included. Secondly, comments should be made on any aspects of the passage that are significant to the novel as a whole, whether in matters relating to themes or to the author's technique.

Example 1. Place the following passage from *Sense and Sensibility* in its context:

'And the bulk of your fortune would be laid out in annuities on the authors or their heirs.'

'No, Edward, I should have something else to do with it.'

'Perhaps then you would bestow it as a reward on that person who wrote the ablest defence of your favourite maxim, that no one can ever be in love more than once in their life—for your opinion on that point is unchanged, I presume?'

'Undoubtedly. At my time of life opinions are tolerably fixed. It is not likely that I should now see or hear anything to change them.'

Answer: This passage is taken from Volume I of *Sense and Sensibility*, and presents a conversation between Marianne Dashwood and Edward Ferrars during the latter's first visit to Mrs Dashwood and her daughters after their departure from Norland. Elinor, Mrs Dashwood and Margaret are also present, and this conversation is part of a general discussion (initiated by Margaret) on the subject of what they would each do with a large fortune. Marianne has just said she would spend part of her money on music and books, and this provokes Edward's joke that she would probably spend the rest of it in annual grants to authors and their children (so that music and literature should be kept alive). Before the chapter ends, Marianne has criticised what she calls Elinor's 'doctrine' of sense, and has drawn general attention to Edward's 'reserve'.

This passage sets in motion Jane Austen's analysis of a favourite THEME, the process by which experience matures and educates the human personality. Marianne believes no person can love a second time, and thinks (wrongly) that her belief is a mature, considered judgement. Jane Austen IRONICALLY has her state that 'at my time of life opinions are ... fixed': the PLOT as it progresses will show Marianne maturing in years and experience, getting over the betrayal of her first love for Willoughby, and finding happiness in a 'second attachment' to Colonel Brandon. The feeling she expresses is typical of her romantic nature, and it is one of the novel's thematic interests to demonstrate how Marianne gradually learns from Elinor how to master this romanticism or 'SENSIBILITY'. Marianne is frequently the object of Jane Austen's SATIRE in the novel, especially in her tearful farewell to the woods at Norland in the novel's early stages, but she is soon seen to develop into a personality in her own right. The speakers in this passage are related to each other: Edward is Marianne's brother-in-law, and the novel's plot centres upon visits paid and letters written between their families and the families of their friends. 'Three or four Families in a Country Village is the very thing to work upon', wrote Jane Austen about the choice of a SETTING for the type of novel she liked writing, and *Sense and Sensibility* illustrates this aspect of her characteristic method. Her characters are true, both to life and to the restricted upper-class society she knew, and through such conversations as the one given in this passage and numerous social meetings in Dorsetshire and in London, Jane Austen explores her themes and voices her criticism of society.

Marianne's love of music and books illustrates the aesthetic side of her sensitive CHARACTER. She feels strongly about art and artists, and in this novel is the chosen representative of the eighteenth-century concept of 'sensibility', the capacity for intense feeling. Edward, on the other hand, represents (with Elinor) 'sense'. He has deep feelings, but will be guided in his actions (again like Elinor) by a sense of duty and responsibility to others. As the novel will reveal in time, the gravity and reserve in his manner that the quick-sighted Marianne notices, is caused by the fact that he has already developed a 'second attachment' (to Elinor), but is restrained from speaking of it to her by his duty to Lucy Steele and his knowledge of his mother's expectations for him. The conversation, which seems to centre on Marianne, has a hidde1 relevance to Edward, who will also mature into independence of spirit before the story is done.

The passage illustrates Jane Austen's ability to handle lifelike, realistic DIALOGUE. The conversation flows along with apparent naturalness, yet the topics discussed simultaneously help the plot along and illuminate the author's main interests. The speeches are entirely in CHARACTER; it is typical of Marianne that she speaks with such decided firmness on all matters, and also characteristic of Edward in his lighter moods that he teases her gently. His teasing is always welcome to Marianne (despite her habitual prickliness and sensitivity) because he shows his respect for her as an individual, and his understanding of her mind. Jane Austen contrasts Edward's teasing with that of Sir John Middleton, whose crudeness and stupidity constantly affront Marianne.

The quiet sparring of Edward and Marianne here balances the warm relationship that will later develop between Elinor and Colonel Brandon. The continual comparison and contrast of Elinor and Marianne are part of the novel's STRUCTURE, and just as Edward's teasing brings out an attractively comic side of Marianne's 'sensibility', so the Colonel's account of his past experiences will exercise Elinor's sympathy and widen her knowledge of the world. Incidents and characters, balanced in this way, unify the novel, which would otherwise provide as unwieldy a tale and cast of characters as any novel by Trollope or Dickens.

Edward's amusement at Marianne's romantic notions is reminiscent of *Northanger Abbey*, Jane Austen's last published novel (but one of her first planned), in which Henry Tilney gently teases Catherine Morland out of her fascination for Gothic horrors and introduces her to a real-life hero. Conversation in an Austen novel is usually quite as exciting and interesting as the action in other novels of the period, for conversation is the principal means by which her characters come to understand each other better, or (as happens in this novel, between Elinor and Lucy Steele) cruelly maim one another. To converse well was one of the cultivated arts of the age, and the fact that such a wide-ranging conversation as this takes place at Barton Cottage, while no talk of any depth or interest can be conducted either at Barton Park or at Mr and Mrs John Dashwood's London house, illustrates Jane Austen's view of her SOCIETY as being, with very few exceptions, dull, uncultured and trivial.

Example 2. Place the following passage in its context:

'. . . You may guess, after all these expenses, how very far we must be from being rich, and how acceptable Mrs Ferrars's kindness is.'

'Certainly,' said Elinor; 'and assisted by her liberality, I hope you may yet live to be in easy circumstances.'

'Another year or two may do much towards it,' he gravely replied; 'but however there is still a great deal to be done. There is not a stone laid of Fanny's greenhouse, and nothing but the plan of the flower-garden marked out.'

'Where is the greenhouse to be?'

'Upon the knoll behind the house. The old walnut trees are all come down to make room for it. It will be a very fine object from many parts of the park, and the flower-garden will slope down just before it, and be exceedingly pretty. We have cleared away all the old thorns that grew in patches over the brow.'

Elinor kept her concern and her censure to herself; and was very thankful that Marianne was not present, to share the provocation.

Answer: This passage is taken from Volume II, and presents part of a conversation between Elinor Dashwood and her stepbrother John as they walk from Mrs Jennings's house to call on the Middletons (to whom John wants Elinor to introduce him). By 'all these expenses', John Dashwood means the expenses of London life, of making alterations at Norland (Elinor's former home), and of replacing with new the household effects that had been left to Elinor's mother on Mr Henry Dashwood's death. These statements are intended to discourage his sister from expecting him to give her and Marianne a brotherly gift! Before the conversation ends, Dashwood has demonstrated his insensitivity and his mercenary nature by congratulating Elinor on having such a wealthy friend as Mrs Jennings, and on having a better chance of a wealthy marriage since her sister Marianne's looks have been ruined by illness. By letting John Dashwood find Lady Middleton a suitable associate for his wife, Jane Austen sets the stage for further meetings between the Dashwoods and the Middletons which will bring about the novel's climax: the revelation, at the beginning of Volume III, of Lucy's engagement to Edward Ferrars.

The passage illustrates Jane Austen's awareness that MONEY often assumed greater significance than natural or human feeling in the society of eighteenth-century England: selfish John Dashwood rates unnecessary and trivial expenses more important than the giving of a present to the two sisters whose former income he and his family are now enjoying. A similar insensitivity to matters of aesthetic taste is evident in his description of the alterations at Norland, where old and beautiful trees have been chopped down to accommodate a mere greenhouse for rearing plants in artificial warmth, and old thorn trees cleared to make room for a formal flower garden. Landscape gardeners usually placed fine statuary or a building modelled on antique Greek lines in a position where it could be admired 'from many parts of' an extensive park (a good example of this can still be seen at Rousham, near Oxford), but John Dashwood and his wife will destroy old trees and give this commanding position to a mere greenhouse! Marianne, as a lover of the natural, the romantic and the picturesque (and as a special devotee of Norland's woods) would have been annoyed and saddened by this so-called 'improvement' of her old home, and unlike the polite and self-controlled Elinor, would have forcefully expressed her feelings. In this way Jane Austen contrasts Elinor's caution and good SENSE with Marianne's SENSIBILITY (a major thematic interest of the novel), and at the same time mirrors the stupid tastelessness of Mr and Mrs Dashwood, who attempt to follow FASHION in improving their property and go about it in ignorance.

Elinor's part in the conversation illustrates her great politeness and (since John Dashwood's words naturally must remind her of the harm his wife's selfishness has done to her mother and sisters) admirable self-control. It also shows her defending her self-respect by means of IRONY: in her superficially polite speech she is actually taunting him as a liar and a hypocrite, and secretly venting her anger by doing so. But he is so stupid and pompous that he takes her words at their face value; and probably congratulates himself secretly that innocent, unworldly Elinor has no idea that she has been treated unjustly by him. It is clear from the last sentence in the passage that Jane Austen shares Elinor's feelings about John and Fanny Dashwood, and expects the reader to share them too. The novel is, as a whole, narrated from Elinor's point of view, although in its early drafts Jane Austen experimented with the epistolary style which permits narration from many points of view.

It is characteristic of Jane Austen that these exchanges, which lay bare the selfishness at the root of John Dashwood's nature and the moral strength that guides Elinor, take place in the course of performing that inevitable part of social life, the payment of a formal call. There is no detail of ordinary life in her time that Jane Austen does not seem able to include in the SETTINGS of her novels in such a way that the most seemingly trivial incidents and objects take on importance and signifi-cance, becoming the means by which she voices her moral concern or SATIRISES the moral flaws of contemporary society.

John Dashwood is such a pattern of self-important stupidity that his CHARACTERISATION comes close to caricature. His thoughtless cruelty makes the reader feel Elinor's anger in his own heart, but the use of the word 'gravely' communicates Jane Austen's amusement at his stupidity, and in the end we laugh at and even pity him, far more than we dislike or hate him. His appearances in the novel, whether in dialogue (as here) or in such description as Mrs Jennings's unforgettable retelling of the scene of Anne's betrayal of Lucy's secret engagement, are rich in comic value, and help to lighten the general effect of a novel which comes, at some points, very close to disaster and tragedy.

John Dashwood's conversation with the intelligent, yet self-controlled Elinor recalls the famous exchange in *Pride and Prejudice* between the equally pompous and stupid Mr Collins and Elizabeth Bennet. Characters such as John Dashwood, Mr Collins, Mrs Ferrars, Lady Catherine de Bourgh (in *Pride and Prejudice*) and Sir Walter Elliot (in *Persuasion*) stand in Jane Austen's novels for the insensitive and mercenary views which she knew dominated much of society in her time. The personal triumphs of an Elinor Dashwood, an Elizabeth Bennet or an Anne Elliot symbolise the occasional victories won by wit, sympathy and virtue in their endless battle with stupidity, pride, and squalid morality.

There are significant details in the passage that seem to mark Jane Austen as a 'transitional' writer. Her management of dialogue reminds us, in its wit and easy flow (and especially in its occasional irony), of Congreve's plays. She reveals an eighteenth-century inheritance in other ways, too, notably in her PHRASING, and in the kind of serious MORAL CONCERN that the novel's main plot and themes express. Like Dr Johnson, Jane Austen appears to have believed that the function of literature was to instruct by pleasing, and even her most comic passage is not without a serious import. On the other hand, although her satire of Marianne's sensibility is also undertaken in the spirit of a true descendant of Pope and Fielding, this is a passage (like later sympathetic descriptions of Marianne's emotional distress) that shows Jane Austen's sympathy for 'romantic' interest in the old, the beautiful, and the picturesque.

When answering context questions, keep the given passage firmly in view, and draw from your summary only those points that can logically be connected with details in the passage. You will find below a number of passages suggested for practice in answering context questions. Some remarks and suggestions accompany a few of these, but as you gain experience you will find that you can do without such aids.

Volume 1, Chapter 1: 'Elinor saw, with concern . . . to similar forbearance.' (Theme of sense versus sensibility; chararacterisation of Elinor, through description and action, if not through her own words; Jane Austen's skill in handling large groups of people exemplified in her creation of a family likeness between Marianne and Mrs Dashwood . . .)

Volume I, Chapter 2: 'Do but consider, my dear Mr Dashwood ... give *you* something.' (Misuse of sense, and absence of sensibility in John and Fanny Dashwood, who put selfish concern for money before family affection and duty. Admirable characterisation of Fanny through her speech: note tone, and diction, careful timing and deployment of arguments, her play on familiar weaknesses in John Dashwood's character . . .)

Volume III, Chapter 14: 'The whole of Lucy's behaviour . . . time and conscience.' (Jane Austen's realism in letting Lucy gain material prosperity; moral condemnation apparent through the superficially matter-of-fact manner and tone; good example of Austen's satiric irony at its most bitter . . .)

Volume III, Chapter 2: 'Very well indeed! . . . great credit.' (Mrs Jennings's remarks track her progress in reading Lucy's letter, a good example of Jane Austen's ability to dramatise an incident and characterise a personality through speech; since we have already seen the letter, the passage reminds us of Lucy's cunning hypocrisy and Mrs Jennings's kindly generosity; ironic comment on society that a literary form such as a letter should be the means by which one ignorant and unrefined woman misleads another . . .)

Volume I, Chapter 3: 'Edward is very amiable . . . indifference!'

Volume I, Chapter 5: 'Dear, dear Norland! ... to enjoy you?'

Volume I, Chapter 7: 'Sir John was a sportsman . . . of his wife.'

Volume I, Chapter 7: 'Colonel Brandon alone . . . which humanity required.'

Volume I, Chapter 9: 'And what sort of a young man . . . shades of his mind.' (Satire, not only at Sir John's expense, but at Marianne's too . . .)

Volume I, Chapter 9: 'That is an expression ... ancles.'

Volume I, Chapter 10: 'In Mrs Dashwood's estimation ... in its support.'

Volume I, Chapter 16: 'The evening passed off ... used to read together.'

Volume I, Chapter 16: '"Oh!" cried Marianne . . . but *sometimes* they are.'

Volume III, Chapter 5: '. . . I could not believe it . . . half frantic.'

Volume I, Chapter 22: 'You may well be surprised . . . quite as his own sisters.'

Volume II, Chapter 7: 'Exert yourself, dear Marianne ... what I suffer.'

Volume III, Chapter 1: '"Well!" said Mrs Jennings . . . feel for him sincerely.'

Volume III, Chapter 8: '. . . Affecting that air of playfulness . . . I am talking like a fool.'

General questions

(1) How does Jane Austen voice her moral convictions through her handling of plot and character?

(2) Do you consider 'Sense and Sensibility' to be an appropriate title for this novel?

(3) In what ways to you consider Jane Austen to be a writer representative of her age?

(4) What aspects of the novel would you take into account in order to establish a reliable idea (a) of Jane Austen's interest in writing fiction, and (b) of her ideas regarding the essentials for a happy marriage?

(5) Discuss the view that *Sense and Sensibility* is (a) a fictionalised moral tract, (b) a satire upon the contemporary cult of 'sensibility', (c) the personal testament of a lonely and resentful spinster, (d) a work of art.

Questions that focus on particular aspects of Jane Austen's achievement

(1) Distinguish between 'character' and 'caricature' in the novel.

(2) Consider Jane Austen's ironic approach to (a) character, and (b) narrative in *Sense and Sensibility*.

(3) What part is played by satire in the scheme of this novel as a whole?

(4) Do you consider Jane Austen's choice of setting for this novel a limitation upon her art?

(5) Comment on some interesting aspects of Jane Austen's approach to language in *Sense and Sensibility*.

(6) Do you think *Sense and Sensibility* would have made a good play? Give reasons for your answer.

(7) What kinds of comedy do you distinguish in this novel?

(8) Compare the respective characterisations of the following:
  (a) Edward Ferrars and John Willoughby
  (b) John Dashwood and Sir John Middleton
  (c) Elinor Dashwood and Marianne Dashwood
  (d) Mrs Jennings, Mrs Henry Dashwood, and Mrs Ferrars
  (e) Colonel Brandon and John Willoughby
  (f) Lucy Steele, Fanny Dashwood, and Lady Middleton
  (g) Anne Steele and Mrs Palmer

(9) How does the structure of the novel show the care with which Jane Austen wrote her fiction?

(10) Demonstrate, through careful analysis of a short passage of your choice, what you consider to be Jane Austen's chief claims to greatness as a writer.

(11) Write a character study of one of the following:
  (a) Elinor Dashwood
  (b) Lucy Steele
  (c) Fanny Dashwood
  (d) John Dashwood

NOTE: See Part 3 of these Notes for suggestions on the writing of this type of answer, and a specimen character study of Marianne Dashwood.

___

Questions that test knowledge of the plot

(1) Comment on the frequency of coincidence in the novel (for example, in the Eliza Williams sub-plot, and in the Steeles happening to be relations of Lady Middleton); how, in your opinion, does it affect the plot?
(2) How well do you think Jane Austen has interwoven sub-plots and main plot?
(3) Comment on the usefulness to the plot of the following characters: Anne Steele; Mr and Mrs Palmer; Sir John and Lady Middleton; Mrs Jennings.
(4) Comment on the usefulness to the plot of the following incidents: (a) Mrs Jennings's misunderstanding of Colonel Brandon's offer of a living to Edward Ferrars (b) Mrs Dashwood's servant's misunderstanding of Lucy Ferrars's message (c) Mrs Dashwood's refusal to question Marianne on the subject of her relationship with Willoughby, and (d) the birth of a child to Mrs Palmer.
(5) How, from your reading of other novels by Jane Austen, would you say increasing maturity affects this novelist's handling of her plots?

NOTE: See pages 81–4 for twenty-five questions designed to test readers' knowledge of the plot (as well as other aspects) of *Sense and Sensibility*, volume by volume and in a survey of the novel as a whole. Here too, as in answering general questions and questions on particular aspects of technique and style, your summary will serve you well.

___

Questions on background

(1) What marks, if any, does the novel bear of the period of its composition?
(2) How accurate do you consider is Jane Austen's picture in *Sense and Sensibility* of the social life of her time?
(3) Discuss the view that Jane Austen is a 'transitional' writer, that is, that her novels bridge the eighteenth and nineteenth centuries.
(4) What evidence does the novel yield regarding Jane Austen's characteristic methods of composition?

(5) Do you consider (*a*) Mrs Ferrars, (*b*) Mrs Jennings, (*c*) Lady Middleton, (*d*) Lucy Steele to be true to life as it was lived by women of Jane Austen's time?

(6) What light does *Sense and Sensibility* shed on the statement that 'the ownership of land was the greatest social asset of the eighteenth century'?

(7) What evidence have you gathered from (*a*) Mrs Dashwood's daughters, (*b*) Edward and Robert Ferrars, (*c*) Anne and Lucy Steele, and (*d*) Lady Middleton and Mrs Palmer, regarding the education of young people in Jane Austen's time?

NOTE: In answering this type of question, draw the information you need on historical, social or textual matters from divisions (g) to (k) in your prepared summary. For material yielded by the novel, refer to the main body of your summary.

Revision questions on Volume I

(1) What knowledge do we gain of the characters of John and Fanny Dashwood from their conversations as reported in Chapter 2?

(2) Do you consider Elinor and Marianne Dashwood convincing examples of girls aged nineteen and seventeen?

(3) Mention some of the ways in which Jane Austen satirises the cult of 'sensibility' through Marianne.

(4) What aspects of her society does Jane Austen satirise through her portraits of (*a*) Sir John and Lady Middleton, and (*b*) John and Fanny Dashwood?

(5) In what ways are family resemblances established between
(*a*) Mrs Henry Dashwood and Marianne
(*b*) Mrs Ferrars and Fanny Dashwood
(*c*) Mrs Jennings and Mrs Palmer
(*d*) Anne and Lucy Steele?

(6) Do you think that Elinor's unfailing politeness sometimes makes her guilty of deceit and hypocrisy?

Revision questions on Volume II

(1) How do (*a*) the making of a filigree basket by Elinor and Lucy, (*b*) the writing of a letter by Willoughby, and (*c*) the dropping of a curtsy by Mrs Ferrars help to reveal character in Volume II?

(2) By what means does Jane Austen lead the reader to revise his first impressions of Mrs Jennings?

(3) Why do you think Jane Austen chose to end Volume I with Elinor's discovery of Edward's engagement to Lucy, and Volume II with Elinor's conviction that the engagement will soon be announced?

(4) What kind of picture do you draw from John Dashwood's speech and behaviour in Chapter 11 of eighteenth-century society's attitude to money?

(5) You have probably noticed that the account of such sensational events as a tragic death, a seduction, a betrayal and a duel has been pressed into a single chapter (9), while a description and analysis of Elinor's reactions as Lucy confides to her the story of her engagement to Edward are spread over three (Volume I, Chapter 22; Volume II, Chapters 1 and 2). Does this fact lead you to any conclusions regarding the nature of Jane Austen's principal interest in writing fiction?

(6) How do their respective styles of speaking and/or writing help to characterise Marianne, Lucy Steele, Mrs Jennings and Robert Ferrars?

(7) What conclusions would you draw from reading Volume II regarding Jane Austen's views on (a) young ladies' 'accomplishments', (b) public school education, (c) patronage in the Church of England, (d) the etiquette of London social life, and (e) the divisions of social rank in the society of her time?

(8) Do you think Jane Austen has succeeded in making Colonel Brandon a worthy and interesting character?

Revision questions on Volume III

(1) Read Mrs Jennings's account of Anne Steele's revelation in Chapter 1, and compare it with Colonel Brandon's account of Elizabeth Brandon and Eliza Williams in Volume II, Chapter 9. Which do you consider more interesting, and why?

(2) How does Jane Austen use the behaviour of (a) Mrs Jennings, (b) Fanny Dashwood, and (c) Lucy Ferrars, to their poor relations and friends, to characterise them?

(3) Compare Mr and Mrs Palmer with Anne Steele (a) as comic characters, and (b) with regard to their other functions (if any) in the novel.

(4) (a) 'There was always a something, if you remember, in Willoughby's eyes at times, which I did not like.'
   (b) 'She is a good-hearted girl as ever lived!'
   (c) 'Poor Edward! His manners are certainly not the happiest in nature.'
   What do these remarks, made by Mrs Henry Dashwood, Mrs Jennings, and Robert Ferrars respectively about other characters in the novel, tell us of their own personalities?

(5) How would you use such phrases as '[Elinor] watched his eyes' in Chapter 6, and '[Edward spoiled] both them and their sheath by

cutting the latter to pieces as he spoke' in Chapter 12 to illustrate Jane Austen's famous description of her art as paintings of life in miniature?

(6) Reread Chapter 10. In what ways have her experiences matured Marianne?

(7) What do Lucy's two letter, written to Elinor and to Edward, tell us of her character?

(8) Basing your statements upon your reading of the novel as a whole, and Volume III in particular, say what you consider Jane Austen believed essential equipment for a happy marriage.

(9) In what ways do Jane Austen's final arrangements for Marianne, Willoughby, and Lucy Steele respectively, challenge the conventions of the romantic novel of sentiment and 'sensibility'?

(10) Reread Chapters 3 and 4, and Chapter 11. Could the complications caused by Mrs Jennings's misunderstanding of Elinor's interview with the Colonel, and the Dashwoods' servant's misunderstanding of Lucy's message have been omitted without very much affecting the novel?

(11) Would you say that, all in all, Jane Austen has drawn a convincing character in Willoughby?

Part 5

Suggestions for further reading

The text

An easily available edition of *Sense and Sensibility* is that in the Penguin English Library, edited by Tony Tanner, Penguin Books, Harmondsworth, 1969 and subsequent reprintings.

The definitive edition of Jane Austen's collected novels is *The Novels of Jane Austen: The Text based on Collation of the Early Editions*, edited by R.W. Chapman, The Clarendon Press, Oxford, 6 vols., 1923–54.

Critical studies

LASCELLES, MARY: *Jane Austen and Her Art*, The Clarendon Press, Oxford and New York, 1939. A sympathetic early study of Jane Austen's fiction.

GOONERATNE, YASMINE: *Jane Austen*, Cambridge University Press, Cambridge, 1970. A critical introduction to Jane Austen's writings.

WRIGHT, ANDREW: *Jane Austen's Novels: A Study in Structure*, Chatto and Windus, London and New York, revised edn, 1964. A useful exploration of aspects of Jane Austen's fiction.

LEAVIS, F.R.: *The Great Tradition*, Chatto and Windus, London, 1948. In the first chapter reasons are given for this critic's placing Jane Austen at the head of the list of 'great English novelists'.

Jane Austen: A Collection of Critical Essays, edited by Ian Watt, Prentice-Hall, Englewood Cliffs, New Jersey, 1963. This collection includes influential modern criticism, particularly that of D.W. Harding.

SOUTHAM, B.C.: *Jane Austen's Literary Manuscripts: A Study of the Novelist's Development through the Surviving Papers*, Oxford University Press, London, 1964. A detailed analysis of extant manuscript material that illuminates Jane Austen's methods of writing, and reveals the craftsmanlike way in which she regarded her work.